"Rest assured, I'm not the sort of man who can abandon a woman in need. If I have the power to do so, I'll be sure to use it."
"Ugh... Claes!"
MW00827763

Luxuria Luscharity
The dark god of lust who faces off with Loren and Lapis. A lover unburdened by gender or age. From grannies and gaffers with a foot in the grave to... nothing worth talking about.
"Just try it. I'll teach you just how powerless mere hunger is before love."
An unignorable level of tension stretched between the two dark gods.

"I could always use force."
Gula
The dark god of gluttony, who appeared before Loren and Lapis when they were in a pinch. She holds authority over all that which may be devoured.

"You're outrageous, Mr. Loren."
Lapis was struck with wonder, but that didn't mean she was down for the count. No matter how powerful Loren's attack had been, Lapis had successfully blocked it.

THE Strange Adventure OF A Broke MERCENARY

The Strange Adventure of a Broke Mercenary

NOVEL

6

WRITTEN BY

Mine

ILLUSTRATED BY

peroshi

Seven Seas Entertainment

KUITSUME YOHEI NO GENSO KITAN Volume 6

Illustrations by peroshi
Originally published in Japan by HOBBY JAPAN, Tokyo.
English translation rights arranged with HOBBY JAPAN, Tokyo, through TOHAN CORPORATION, Tokyo.

Seven Seas press and purchase enquiries can be sent to Marketing Manager Lianne Sentar at press@gomanga.com. Information regarding the distribution and purchase of digital editions is available from Digital Manager CK Russell at digital@gomanga.com.

Follow Seven Seas Entertainment online at sevenseasentertainment.com.

TRANSLATION: Roy Nukia
ADAPTATION: N. Candon
COVER DESIGN: H. Qi
INTERIOR LAYOUT & DESIGN: Clay Gardner
COPY EDITOR: Jehanne Bell
PROOFREADER: Meg van Huygen
LIGHT NOVEL EDITOR: E.M. Candon
PREPRESS TECHNICIAN: Jules Valera
PRODUCTION MANAGER: Lissa Pattillo
EDITOR-IN-CHIEF: Julie Davis
ASSOCIATE PUBLISHER: Adam Arnold
PUBLISHER: Jason DeAngelis

ISBN: 978-1-63858-595-4
Printed in Canada
First Printing: October 2022
10 9 8 7 6 5 4 3 2 1

THE STRANGE ADVENTURE OF A BROKE MERCENARY

Fantasie Geshichte von Söldner in großer Armut

CONTENTS

Prologue
From Investigation to Outbreak

THE RUMOR WAS SPREADING—somewhere in the world, several villages had been wiped off the map.

That wasn't anything rare. New settlements often sprouted up only to be destroyed. Nowadays, they were simply rebuilt on the site of their destruction, so there was never much fuss when someone laid waste to a handful of villages.

However, this situation was a bit different. As it turned out, there was another rumor going around hand in hand with this one—that these villages had been destroyed by a blood blight. A blood blight, of course, referred to any calamity brought about by a vampire.

A vampire might appear in a human settlement and take a few of its members as servants. Those servants would go on to attack other humans, thereby turning the wheel of a truly bloody and tragic cycle until an entire region was left devoid of life, all the humans replaced by throngs of undead.

This, in turn, produced a great undead army of such scale that even a nation couldn't ignore it. It was quite serious, even when it was only whispered rumor. The country in question had immediately mobilized to investigate.

"Not that I think they'll be finding any undead armies," Lapis muttered, as if it didn't concern her.

Loren stared at the girl sitting across from him as he lazily tilted his glass of ale and let the liquid slowly swirl.

Lapis was right; in all likelihood, those pesky undead from all those fallen villages would never be found. This insight didn't spring from some divine revelation Lapis had received in her role as a priest to the god of knowledge. Rather, it had to do with a job he and she had taken not too long ago.

Their quest hadn't been processed through the guild, and had instead been a direct request from a client. Those villages had been decimated specifically to create an army of undead to assault Loren and Lapis in the midst of this quest, and nearly all of the undead thus produced had been exterminated—likely alongside the vampires who had been ultimately responsible for the blood blight.

They'd never reported this to the guild. If the adventurers' guild wanted to know about it, Loren figured they should ask the Elders, who stood above all other vampires. He knew the guild was mighty in its own right; it had ways of communicating with the sorts of monsters that could reach common ground with humans. If it hadn't had those ways, there was no way they could've learned a number of the things they'd known in the past. In any case, the whole mess was over now, and there was no use thinking about it.

Given that he and Lapis done all their own client negotiation for that one, they had no obligation to report anything about the mission to the guild in the first place. If they kept silent, and the Elders didn't say anything either, that was the end of that.

Surely the guild knew something was up, but the organization couldn't carelessly pick a fight with the Elders. Nor could they risk upsetting a cabal of powerful vampires by forcing said vampire's contractors to cough up any secrets.

That's why I reckon the guild's overlooking the whole thing for now, thought Loren. "I feel sorry for the sad saps they sent to hunt 'em down."

Nothing would come of it no matter how much the guild dug into it. The Elders had retreated, while the undead army had fallen to either Loren or the sun. The dead returned to the earth. Loren found the thought of a fruitless investigation quite terrible, but the investigators would be paid their daily rate regardless. He sent a prayer up for whatever adventurers were on the task, hoping they wouldn't find it as mind-numbing as he would.

"But that's the least of our worries right now," Loren groaned as he lowered his eyes to the notice spread over the table. This particular notice had been handed out to every adventurer in the guild—its contents so profound that it had nearly driven all thoughts of vampires, zombie hordes, and undead dragon innards right out of Loren's head.

"It might just be skirmishes for now, but it's still an official war," said Lapis who, unlike Loren, sounded terribly uninterested.

The paper informed them that Waargenberg, the nation that laid claim to the town of Kaffa, had officially entered a war with Schoenbryn to its north on some nameless plain near the border. The guild's notice didn't spare a single word for what had instigated the battle, but Loren knew from experience: *It's not like it's going to be any decent reason anyway.*

Wars rarely ever started for an interesting reason. They generally broke out over incredibly pointless things, so he didn't really care about the related politics. The problem was that these skirmishes had halted trade, and soldiers were being called up from towns and villages all over. This meant that there would be fewer soldiers around to maintain the peace, and public order was on the decline.

"On its most fundamental level, the guild is supposed to maintain neutrality," said Lapis.

But though the organization itself claimed neutrality, that didn't mean that they could scoop up quests on both sides of the war. Here, the board was flooded with quests from Waargenberg: some to scope out the area around the battlefield, others to guard key personnel, and more to guard bases and forts, as well as a few for handling general military duties.

The situation was likely mirrored in Schoenbryn, and the adventurers would be all astir with this sudden influx of work.

"Is your mercenary blood boiling?" Lapis asked brazenly.

Loren pondered that question for a moment. "Not interested. Don't feel the slightest urge to join in. Also, I'm a *former* mercenary."

"But don't you think this sounds incredibly profitable? It might be your time to shine."

Not long ago, Loren had believed he would be able to immediately pay back his debts the moment war broke out. However, now that it had actually happened, he realized he wasn't that keen on it. He lifted his glass and downed it in one breath. "Yeah, it's not doing it for me. I'm fine where I am right now."

And that was the end of that when it came to his feelings on the matter. At the very least, his current lifestyle was easier and safer than the days he'd spent on his toes at every waking moment. It was certainly better than never knowing when an enemy attack would come, or wandering battlefields without a decent meal or place to sleep.

With his new job, he often met dangers that outstripped any war, but he was somehow still alive and felt no right to complain.

"That's a little encouraging to hear," Lapis smiled a bit, shifting slightly in her seat as if to conceal the act. Loren felt a bit awkward meeting her gaze and found himself shifting as well to escape it.

Lapis seemed a little displeased by that. However, she quickly bounced back with a new topic. "In that case, we won't take any quests related to the war... Though that really limits our choices."

The nation was blessing them with an endless supply of well-paying jobs, but those jobs would drown out any other work, which the guild probably wouldn't even bother to promote. After all, though the guild served as a sort of mutual-aid network for adventurers, the organization itself was out to make a profit.

With so many profitable jobs flying around, they naturally wouldn't go out of their way to invest time in chump change.

"Mr. Loren, do you have the savings to wait out a war?"

This sudden question extracted a deeply unpleasant face from Loren. That was the first of a whole host of questions he didn't want to answer.

"You know I don't," he bitterly replied.

With all his debts, it was impossible for Loren to save anything at all. The IOUs were all to Lapis—they came with a ridiculous lack of interest or any real incentive for him to pay her back. However, it wasn't in Loren's character to fill his pockets when he had outstanding loans.

"As I thought. That means you can't stop working entirely, or you'll dry up before the war's over."

"As pathetic as that sounds."

Lately, he had taken to carrying a bit of pocket change. However, a war could last from a few days to far longer; when asked if he had enough to survive the whole while, Loren had to shake his head. He didn't know where he would turn once his pockets were emptied. He would be left to slowly waste away.

"Then we really must work, wouldn't you say?"

He couldn't contradict her once she'd spelled it out for him. Lapis, pouncing on the moment, produced some pieces of paper from the pocket of her robe and spread them over the table.

"There wasn't much I could do. Right now, it's all about the war."

It wasn't that no one wanted to hire folks for normal questing, just that if the guild didn't post the requests, no one would see them. Everything pinned on the overfull board was military-adjacent.

"I did try picking something as unrelated as possible," Lapis continued.

"So you already looked into it..."

She had anticipated all of this in advance and gathered the necessary information. On one hand, it showed her incredible skill at what she did. On the other hand, this was Lapis he was dealing with. Loren couldn't discard the detestable possibility that she had subtly guided him to the conclusions he had just reached. He gave her a sour look.

"Now as for my recommendations..." Lapis paused. "Is something wrong?"

"No, nothing. Go on."

Whether she simply had good foresight or had led him on, that had nothing to do with the next matter on their agenda. Loren gave up on being annoyed and prompted her to speak.

Although Lapis stared at him with a tilt of her head, she swiftly regained herself and began explaining her recommended quests.

THE Strange Adventure OF A Broke MERCENARY

1 A Choice to Depart

THUS, THREE SHEETS OF PAPER were placed before Loren, each a request Lapis had nicked from the bulletin board beside the front desk. She urged him to choose one, and Loren skimmed through the information. When he thought about it, though, perhaps Lapis had a hand in this part of the process as well—would she somehow manipulate his decision? He looked at her, trying to pick up on any sign of a scheme, but she only smiled back, as if to ask him if something was wrong.

He decided not to think about it. Lapis was a demon, one kicked out of her homeland to see the world, and Loren was stuck with her whether he liked it or not. It was a bit too late to worry about her trickery. In any case, getting wound up about it wouldn't change anything.

Loren flipped through the papers, reading each one. While none of them involved joining the front line, each did have a clear connection to the war effort.

"Scoping out an unknown region? Now that's just advance recon, ain't it? I've been put up to that a few times before, and it can be a mess. Sometimes the enemy lays traps for scouts."

This was clearly a mission to map the terrain and state of the battlefield before the fighting began. It was incredibly foolhardy to march an army into combat without adequate information; so long as time permitted, generals would invest a good amount of manpower in discerning the lay of the land. Of course, the same went for the enemy; in most cases, the two scouting forces ended up skirmishing anyway.

Worst-case scenario, those tussles could drag on until the main forces entered the fray, and full-scale warfare would swallow up the scouts. Despite Loren's suspicions, the quest form mentioned nothing of the sort. It simply stated that some region required a general survey. If anyone took that slippery description at face value, the easy-breezy quest could force them into the middle of a long and bloody conflict.

"Guarding the supply units is also a no-go. Cutting off supply lines is a basic tactic. Unless this country has exceptional defenses, there's no question that guarding means fighting. The enemy'll send their swiftest mercenaries... And because it's described as a simple escort job, the pay isn't even that great."

This was more of a logistical support role, so to the untrained eye it probably seemed safer. However, there would be sporadic attacks from small bands of mercenaries along the way. Any successful attack on a caravan would follow the rule of "to the victor go the spoils," so mercenaries were eager to snap up such lucrative gigs. After all, if a company played its cards right, it would be an all-you-can-grab feast of goods, money, and even people. Morale would be high for the attackers, and the danger level would be high as well.

"If a fight unfolds well within your nation's territory, then guard missions can be easy enough...but that's not how it is with this war, right?" Loren asked.

"Yes, correct. The battlefield is to the east of this nation and south of their foe. As for why they're getting all heated up about that region in particular, well, I couldn't even hazard a guess."

"Wait, what's up with that?"

When countries fought, it was safe to assume they were scrabbling for something. In the simplest cases, it was a territorial dispute that saw fighting largely within the borders of one of the nations involved. Yet Lapis made it sound as if they were fighting in a place that didn't belong to anyone. This war was getting curiouser and curiouser.

"The ruckus is kicking up on a flat plain near the center of the continent. The plain is dotted with beast-kind clans, but no nations lay claim to it."

"I don't get the point of that. What are they trying to snatch up all the way out there?"

"When they tried to drive out the beast-kind and cultivate the land, both nations made a grab for the same spot and collided. The sparks from the skirmishes ignited a moderate-sized war, apparently."

In short, they were both aiming for a spot that wasn't recognized as belonging to any human nation. It had originally been the sole domain of beast-kind—which, as far Loren was considered, meant it belonged to beast-kind—but beast-kind were treated with little respect, and it wasn't a shock that their status as landowners was violently disregarded.

"Beast-kind are those odd folks, right? That race that looks human with animal parts stuck onto their bodies here and there?"

"Yes. Some say their race was manufactured by the ancient kingdom."

Evidently, there was a heated, ongoing debate as to whether beast-kind were chimera artificially created from the combination of humans and wild animals. Supporters of the theory claimed beast-kind were the product of research conducted in the days of the ancient kingdom, but not even the beast-kind clans knew the whole truth.

As beast-kind, predictably, possessed the traits of beasts, their feet were fleeter and their arms stronger than those of a human like Loren; in exchange, their lifespans were comparatively short, which lent some credence to the chimera theory.

"Must be a real bother for the people who were living there already."

Lapis shrugged and said dryly, "There aren't any unbothersome wars in the world, Mr. Loren."

Loren looked at the last request. This one was to guard a caravan carrying supplies to a village near the battlefield. "More of the same. There's a high chance we'll get attacked on that one."

This shipment was for a new settlement established a short distance from the war zone. The job involved delivering the villagers their daily necessities, and the supplies were dearly needed.

The village chief making the request had likely gone through hell and high water to secure a merchant willing to brave the danger, and no doubt wished to protect the shipment by hiring guards. This must've cost a pretty penny, but the villagers' lives couldn't be weighed against coin. In which case, even if the rewards were a bit wanting, Loren felt more compelled to take the job.

But as he read more into the details, he found himself grimacing. "Four days to get there, four days back, and it only pays eight silver per person?"

"Since we have to cover our own expenses on top of that, it seems the rewards were too low for anyone else to give it a second glance."

The request would send them into the red even if everything went off without a hitch. Not to mention there was still a high chance of attack, despite the fact that they'd be steering clear of the war.

They would need to gather their necessities and pay for space in the merchant's caravan, all for someone who probably couldn't offer much more reward even if they wanted to.

Who would ever agree to that? Loren thought as he plucked the request out from the pack. "This one's no good, Lapis. Not even up for discussion."

He needed to work or he'd starve, but he wasn't stupid enough to take on a job with no meaningful reward. If he were to keep down the cost as much as possible, perhaps he could eke out a meager profit—but Loren knew that those who were frugal in their preparations were often punished for it.

"A dangerous quest, a deceptively hard quest, and a quest that's not worth the effort. I'd be better off laying around on an empty stomach in Kaffa," he grumbled.

"Oh, no need to be like that," said a new voice without warning. "There's a quest I want you to take, Loren."

Loren turned to glare at its owner. Lapis's face simultaneously twisted in blatant disgust. Though the owner of the voice seemed to pick up on the fact that he wasn't welcome, the red-haired man tried to act indifferent as he set a hand down on their table.

Claes was relatively famous within the guild as a talented adventurer and seemed to be receiving patronage from some country or another. Though he traveled with a party—one with three lovely ladies, no less—he approached Loren and Lapis on his own.

"What are you here for? And what are you plotting?" Lapis demanded.

Claes was unbearable, the sort of person whom Loren had instantly wished to never associate with, following their first meeting. After they'd waded through some crap together, Claes had recognized Loren's abilities and his attitude had improved, but he was still annoying as hell. That being said, Loren didn't completely despise him.

As someone who possessed a special skill known as a "gift," Claes could have made a name for himself as a true hero, given the right circumstances. On the other hand, he was a real philanderer when it came to women, and while he knew his vices, he had yet to show signs of trying to improve himself. That went a long way toward explaining why Lapis treated him so terribly.

"Why would I be plotting anything?" Claes protested. "Against you, no less?"

"That's the right way to think about it. But in that case, why are you butting in on our conversation?"

"I told you at the start. There's a quest I want you to take."

"Do you mean among these?" Lapis pointed at the three sheets on the table, her milk-curdling glare never leaving Claes's face.

Claes nodded briskly. "Why don't you try to guess which?"

"Well, it has to be..."

"Oh, I think I've got it," said Loren. "It's the one to send supplies to the village."

Claes stopped. Realizing Loren had hit the mark, Lapis promptly ignored Claes and curiously turned to Loren.

"Why do you think so?" she asked.

"The other two have to do with the nation's interests; the clients are some big shots in the army. More often than not, that means they're arrogant or sleazy old men."

Loren's opinion sounded incredibly biased, but for some reason, Lapis had a vague sense that he was right. At the very least, when a kingdom was involved, their point of contact wasn't likely to be some affable young person.

"That leaves the last one, where the client is some village chief."

"Excuse me, Mr. Loren. The way I see it, 'village chief' would be the one most likely to be an old man."

Maybe it was an idea steeped in the wisdom of ages, or maybe something else entirely, but the term "village chief" carried with it a strong mental image. Loren thought so too, but he knew that wasn't all a village chief could be.

"For places that have been around for a long time, the chief is usually an elder who grew up with the village. But sometimes the chief of a new village can be a younger man or woman."

"Perhaps you have a point..."

"And even if they are old, that just means they could have a daughter or granddaughter, right?"

"Oh, I see."

A chief was often rich, at least when compared to the rest of the villagers. It went without saying that they shouldered a responsibility to match, but their riches meant that their daughters or granddaughters were oftentimes well turned out.

And even if a given village were without a charming chief's granddaughter, they'd still have their prettiest woman—and she'd owe both the chief and the supply escort a true debt of gratitude.

"Meaning: it's about women again," Lapis declared, her eyes cold enough to freeze one's soul.

Claes's confident grin immediately transformed into a face of great distress. Without any warning, he clung onto Loren's hands and pleaded in a pitiful voice. "I'm begging you, Loren! I'll even pay a bonus out of my own pocket! Just hear me out here!"

"I'll be honest. I really don't want to do this," Loren muttered. "I'm getting a terrible feeling about this..."

"You're the only one I can count on!"

Loren tried to shake Claes's hands off, but Claes gripped with a surprising amount of strength. As he was unable to squirm away, Loren used his free hand to push back Claes's encroaching face.

"Bastard... You're using *Boost*?! I don't know where your hands have been! Let go already!"

"I will *never* let go! Not until you hear what I have to tell you!"

"Don't phrase it in a way that could cause misunderstandings!" Loren yelled. He shoved a leg between them to push Claes off, but Claes clung desperately.

Lapis passively watched from her front-row seat. She soon began to wonder if she should help get the situation under control or if it would be more interesting to see how things panned out.

Once Loren had managed to tear him away, Claes regained some of his composure. Now a bit more settled, he started in on his offer.

"If you take the job, I'll pay you five silver in advance, and another five on completion."

"Would that be per person?" Lapis asked.

"Erk... O-of course. Twenty silver in total. Not a bad deal, right?"

"Not happening."

Lapis's question had made Claes a little hopeful, but Loren was quick to snatch away his enthusiasm. He still showed no interest, ending the conversation before it could even begin.

Lapis looked at him curiously, so Loren begrudgingly explained himself. "Don't ever trust a job if the first thing they do is try to hook you with cash. The suckers who fall for that kind of thing are the ones who don't last long."

"I see. Then we're done with him," Lapis said in a bone-chilling tone as she pointed at Claes.

Loren had been pulling quite the harsh face himself, but he faltered in the face of Lapis's glower. "Well...we could at least hear him out."

"Whose side are you on?" Lapis's voice stiffened at his indecisiveness.

"It's just..." Loren wasn't usually one to wheedle, so was quite the marked change from his usual attitude. "Well, you know. As long as the terms are good enough, I don't think he's the sort of guy who'd throw us to the wolves."

"Mr. Loren. Are you perhaps a bit soft on Mr. Claes?"

"I don't think I'm that soft..." Loren realized he was close to putting himself at a disadvantage in this conversation, and he forcefully changed the subject. "We can talk about that later."

It was a blatant retreat, but Lapis let him get away with it.

"If you're asking for our help, then tell us every last detail," Loren said to Claes. "After that, I'll offer terms that we might be willing to work for."

"I'll give you a little twist every time I smell you lying. As for what I twist, that depends on how angry I am when it happens."

Lapis's threat punctuated Loren's sincerity; Claes rushed headlong into his tale.

"I'm sure you've seen the meager reward on the posting. At first, we didn't want to take a job that would put us in the red either."

"You say 'we.' Then are Ange and the other girls going to be on the job as well?"

Claes was the only man in his party. At first, Loren had thought this was another one of Claes's romantic escapades, and that his party members had stubbornly declined to humor him. He'd met the women of Claes's party a few times; while they all seemed to harbor some romantic inclinations toward him, Claes couldn't hide his boorishness when it came to women. His party members were just as fed up with him as everyone else.

It's about time they lost interest, Loren thought. He wondered if the day had finally come, but that didn't seem to be the case.

"They agreed to pitch in when they heard of the village's struggles."

"Wow, they're easy. So what's really going on?"

"I want you to keep this between us..."

"Your party's love affairs are none of my business." It wasn't Loren's style to air other people's dirty laundry, in any case. Whatever it was, he genuinely didn't care whether Claes's party members found out or not. He simply wanted to know why Claes was going out of his way to rope him into this.

"Well, to be honest, when the chief came to post the quest..."

"Was she young?"

"I wouldn't say that. Rather, I'd say she had a dazzling, mature allure... She was married, but she lost her husband last year..."

"What? Did she beg for help and awaken your desire to protect her or something?"

"And a few other desires, to be honest..."

"Come on. One of these days, this is gonna catch up to you. I hope you don't think you're gonna die peacefully in your sleep." Loren could warn Claes all he wanted, but the kid's life was ultimately his own. How he spent his time and money was none of Loren's business, and neither was his inevitable messy end.

"You know how it is... Ha ha ha..." Claes chuckled, not the least bit taken aback by this blunt prophecy.

Loren scoffed a little, and Lapis let out a deep sigh that she didn't even attempt to conceal.

"So, how about it? Do you think you can help me?" Claes asked.

"The fact you came to us means no other adventurer was too keen on the quest, right?"

"Pretty much. I wouldn't have accepted it if the chief were anyone else," Claes said matter-of-factly.

Where does he get that nerve of his? I'd like to take a page out of his book, Loren thought. He knew that a wise man would tell Claes to go take a long walk off a short cliff. However, as he glared at Claes—the man's eyes overflowing with hope—Loren's mind took a different route instead.

As he'd proved now and many times before, Claes was a young man who could be summed up as "trash," plain and simple. However, there was some small part of the guy that hesitated to abandon those in need. He also the wielded the rare gift *Boost*, and he was an incredibly skilled swordsman—once his personality was taken out of the equation.

Additionally, while it was unknown how much longer they

would put up with Claes, the women who made up the rest of his team were all quite competent in their own right. As a whole, his party was exceedingly skilled.

Claes wasn't the worst person to sell a favor to. Plain old trash might forget a favor, but Claes stopped short of outright dumpster fire.

"We're not strangers," Loren said. "I think I could accept, depending on the reward."

Opinion given, he turned to get Lapis's take. She looked as reluctant as ever, but she didn't seem completely opposed. She nodded. "I think we could come to an agreement, depending on the reward."

"Is twenty silver not good enough?" Claes asked, throwing his initial figure back into the ring.

Loren shook his head. "That won't do it. Not worth the effort."

"We *are* iron rank adventurers now. You will need to pay us accordingly if you want our services."

For some reason, Claes's face lit up. "You got promoted? Congrats!"

"Weren't you the examiner? They never told you the result?"

"It got hazy along the way, and I was left in the dark."

The promotion exam had been staged for Loren to show his skill with the sword, with Claes as his opponent. A certain someone had interrupted the exam partway through, and as Claes said, the whole thing had become a bit muddled. However, for whatever reason, they'd ended up passing and could now proudly carry iron tags.

"You heard her. Our rates have gone up since the promotion."

"Maybe I celebrated too early," Claes groused.

"Just give up. As for my conditions, I'll agree to an advance payment of—"

"Fifteen silver in advance, fifteen after," Lapis cut in. "That adds to thirty per person. If you foot the necessary expenses as well, we'll take the job."

Claes was understandably startled; she had casually thrown out a number three times his initial offer. But anything less than surprise, and maybe a little bit of offense, would have meant he was trying to lowball them.

"Isn't that a bit too high?" he asked, the corners of his lips twitching.

Incidentally, Loren had intended to offer ten silver before and after per person, forty in total. That was already twice what Claes was offering, and Loren had worried that would be overdoing it. Now not only was Lapis demanding more, she shamelessly also insisted that Claes cover their daily expenses.

"I'm not going to force you," said Lapis. "If you don't agree with those conditions, you can try elsewhere."

Lost at sea, Claes turned the puppy-dog eyes to Loren, begging him to do something about Lapis's cold attitude. But it was too late for Loren to send a lifeboat. Lapis had interrupted him to name her price; she was the more experienced adventurer, and her rates were likely more in line with what an iron rank deserved.

If Lapis continued to escalate, Claes would very possibly be left unable to pay. The original quest had only covered a measly eight silver; even if this was all rooted in Claes's skirt-chasing, Loren was beginning to pity him.

"Can you offer a friends and family discount?" Claes asked.

"I believe I've already gone well below market value."

"Be that as it may, I'm not made of money."

"That sounds like more of a you problem."

Lapis's cold tone held steady, but her gaze darted toward Loren. He didn't know exactly what she meant, but he could tell she wanted *something.*

"How about we take it easy, Lapis?" he asked. "We've been through some trouble together. You could cut him a bit of slack."

"You're the leader here, Mr. Loren. I will respect your decisions."

"Fifty silver total and living expenses for the both of us. That's as low as we'll go, Claes."

Loren didn't feel like he had offered much of a discount. However, it wouldn't have been to Claes's benefit to let him off too easy. Regular setbacks in his womanizing nonsense might even teach him an important lesson and tack a few more years onto his lifespan.

<*That sounds kinda pointless, Mister,*> commented the Lifeless King in Loren's head, her tone equally as cold as Lapis's. This king had lost her physical form and rented space in Loren's spirit as an astral body.

As Loren watched Claes lower his head again and again, delighted at this slight markdown, Loren wondered if the women in his life might not be right.

Naturally, Lapis wasn't going to hold back even once Claes said he would cover their daily expenses. Insisting she couldn't trust a verbal agreement, she smoothly drafted up a contract and signed it with a flourish. Formalities out of the way, she swiped a bag of silver off of Claes and began preparing for their departure.

"Should I register for the quest?" Loren asked.

"Not yet. Help me with the shopping first. We will be working with Mr. Claes, so we should register as a part of his party."

If they silently tagged along, they wouldn't be able to claim the reward offered through the guild. It was a pain, and taking such a piddly quest would earn them some strange looks, but they still needed to do the paperwork—or so Loren thought. Lapis intended to have Claes take care of it.

Their acceptance was set in stone now, and Claes patted his chest in relief. "That makes me the leader," he said. "You'll be following my orders."

Isn't that obvious? Loren was about to say.

But upon seeing the warmth drop from Lapis's eyes, Claes hurriedly raised his hands. "Kidding, kidding. I'll register you as party members, but you'll be free to move on your own."

"Make sure you put us down as *temporary* members. If you officially add us, I'll pluck it right off."

I'd better not ask what she means by "it," thought Loren.

Beside him, Claes covered his nether regions with a pale face, nodding frantically.

After this exchange, Loren and Lapis headed out to town for their preparations, having shoved all the troublesome bureaucratic procedures onto Claes.

"We have plenty of funds this time," Lapis said. "It would be a waste not to use this opportunity."

"How about a bit of restraint? If we're stingy, next time we're in trouble, we might not have to get bailed out."

Some expenses were inevitable, but there was a line of excess that just couldn't be crossed. Back in his mercenary days, Loren knew a few mercs who'd gotten their just deserts and found themselves fruitlessly pleading to their fellow squad members for help. On the other hand, though they'd all had their share of painful experiences, very few had been injured beyond recovery.

Mercenaries all fell on hard times at some point in their lives, and so most were willing to help out to make sure a comrade might lose his dignity, but never his life or limb. This sort of give-and-take forged close bonds in a company. Debts were never forgotten; instead of repaying each other tit for tat, a sort of tacit understanding was born, in which everyone would watch each other's back.

Having grown up with this system, Loren wasn't inclined to let Claes reap *everything* he'd sown. Just most of it.

"Do you honestly think we'll ever need to go running to Mr. Claes in tears?" Lapis, for one, clearly did not.

Loren neither nodded nor shook his head; he simply patted her on the shoulder. "There's no guarantee we won't."

"I see. You may be right. Then I shall give up on the two top-tier sleeping bags and goose-down pillows." Preparations were essential to any journey, but their sleeping supplies were in all-right shape and certainly didn't need fancy replacements. Lapis begrudgingly relinquished that dream.

"And just how much were you planning to buy?" Loren retorted helplessly.

Their preparations ended when they had completely exhausted the funds from Claes. The next day, they packed up and headed toward the designated meeting place.

Claes's party, fully prepared, waited for them at Kaffa's east gate. Gathered alongside them were several carts of supplies to bring back to the village. As one might expect, their client, the village chief, awaited them as well.

"You have my sincere gratitude for taking me up on this request," she said with a courteous bow. Her long brown hair was gathered into a careful bun at the back of her skull, and she wore simple but well-tailored clothes. Her figure was so abundant that "well-tailored" meant a *lot* of cloth to contain it, and her ample chest followed her breath and movement.

I see why he fell so easily, Loren thought as he glanced at Claes's slovenly expression.

"Mr. Loren..." Lapis's voice tolled with displeasure.

Loren felt a pressure on his thigh, and he primly shifted his eyes from the chief's chest to her face.

"I'm trusting you on this one, Mr. Loren," Lapis said. "But based on your behavior, I might have to pluck yours off too."

"Now that's a threat if I ever heard one."

Loren's equipment consisted of the leather jacket, gloves, and boots he had received after fulfilling his previous request. His usual large sword was slung over his back. His pants, on the other hand, were simply a sturdy pair he had found at the marketplace.

If Lapis felt like it, she could easily bypass the cloth to flay his flesh from his bones. With no sign yet of her letting go of his thigh, Loren broke into a cold sweat.

"I am the village chief, Rose. I am counting on you to guard this convoy along the way." Rose lowered her head again as she introduced herself.

Claes had absolutely no reservations about staring at her ample chest with a sleazy smile on his face—and it seemed that it was only now that Ange and the rest of his party realized what he was up to. He ate a merciless kick and rolled along the ground.

Taking his eyes off the chief, who seemed taken aback by the ruckus, Loren looked to the other people around the wagons, the residents of Rose's village. Something felt off about the group.

"Mr. Loren? I really will do something I'll regret."

"Yeah, yeah, I'm about to wet myself. Anyways, doesn't something seem strange to you?" The reason Lapis kept threatening him lay in those gathered villagers. "Why are they all women?"

Women tying ropes around the high piles of supplies. Women loading jute bags onto a wagon that still had space to spare. For some reason, all the villagers at work were women. Normally, this sort of hard labor would have at least included men. While the scene before them wasn't completely outside the realm of possibility, something definitely didn't add up.

Perhaps it was because the village chief was a woman. It was possible she was more willing to include women on her crew—but it still wasn't exactly normal for not a single man to be in sight.

"Perhaps they got drafted into the war effort?" Lapis asked, finally realizing what he meant. Releasing Loren's leg, she took a wide look around, but she didn't spy a single fellow.

"You think they're going out of their way to draft men from puny, out-of-the-way settlements? There aren't many men out there to begin with, and they won't offer much for the effort. In exchange, they'd be taking away part of a village's workforce and earning the resentment of all its residents. It's just not worth it. Or at least, I wouldn't do it."

"Then maybe they were too otherwise preoccupied in the village to be sent here?"

"These supplies are the village's lifeline. Can you think of any job more important than getting them?"

"You might have a point."

There had to be some reason for it, but Loren and Lapis were both simply adventurers hired to guard these folk. Rather than sticking their noses where they didn't belong, it was better to put the notion out of their minds. By the time Rose called out to announce that they were ready to go, Loren was ready to ignore any further oddities.

"All right, let's get going. I'm counting on all of you."

The donkeys pulling the wagons started off at once.

In order to devote their undivided attention to keeping watch, Loren left his bags in an open spot on one of the wagons and walked beside it, matching its slow pace.

As soon as he settled in, Ange approached them. "Hi again, Loren. I'm surprised you two accepted a job like this."

Loren couldn't muster a reply. He looked for Claes and found him trying to make himself look smaller, an apologetic grimace on his face as a woman in knight's armor and a lady priest mouthed off complaints behind him.

"You didn't hear anything about this from Claes?" Loren asked her.

Although it was only temporary, they were members of the same party. *At least explain things to your inner circle,* Loren thought. Though with things as they were, perhaps Claes found it difficult to confess.

"No, he didn't tell us any details. If it was going to be like this, I think we would have been better off sending Claes on his own."

"You shouldn't complain about the job when you're on the clock."

"Ah. Sorry."

Regardless of what the job was, they'd agreed to its terms and now they were in it for the long haul. That was true for both mercenaries and adventurers. Of course, Loren understood full well why Ange would want to complain, so he couldn't be too hard on her.

"He just asked us to help out," Loren said. "I don't know much else. I know you have a lot on your mind, but even if his motives were impure, I'm sure a part of him did just want to help out a village in trouble."

Loren knew this was a quest that no smart man would ever take. An idiot, meanwhile, might have been roped in regardless of reward. Claes wasn't an idiot, but he was a lech, and his calculus had probably involved his funds, his libido, and his bleeding heart in equal measure; it certainly wasn't praiseworthy, but it was a fascinating balancing act.

Not that Loren knew if Claes was actually putting that much thought into it. To be perfectly honest, there was a high chance the man was simply blinded by lust, but telling Ange that would only make things worse. Loren knew absolutely nothing good would come of riling her up.

"Anyways, it's up to you lot to make sure he doesn't take it too far," he said.

"With our fists, feet, swords, and magic, you mean?"

"Why don't you try something a little more peaceable..."

For some reason, Ange already had violence on the mind—though maybe this was just proof of how much pent-up resentment was simmering in Claes's party. Perhaps it was time to give the man a more pointed warning to be more tactful with his party members. As Loren began considering how he might drop such a hint, Lapis posed the big question.

"Why don't you just leave him to his fate?" she asked, sounding genuinely confused.

"Well yeah, that's an option," Loren admitted. "I just think we should avoid tragedies when we can."

"Is that how you see it? I can't shake the feeling that he'll stick his head into the lion's mouth no matter how many times you warn him."

Lapis's opinion of Claes was practically at rock-bottom.

I guess guys and gals take it differently, Loren thought as he decided that would be the end of the conversation. Ange had been listening to their chat with interest. He gave her a pat on the back before turning his attention elsewhere.

THE Strange Adventure OF A Broke MERCENARY

2 Onset to Deviation

FOR SOME TIME, the road out of Kaffa remained peaceful. The first stretch of the journey was along the highway, where patrolling soldiers maintained public order, greatly reducing a caravan's risk. Eventually, however, they would have to leave this safety.

By the second sunset of their four-day journey, Loren began to wonder if the villagers needed any guards at all. Even their nightly campsites seemed quite peaceful.

All of the villagers traveling with Rose were women, as were Claes's and Loren's companions; Loren and Claes were the only men present, and Loren feared it might grow uncomfortably awkward. This turned out not to be the case, as long as he kept his mind on work. He rotated out with Claes's party for the night watch and kept company with Lapis, and only Lapis, during his shifts. In that way, his scenery was no different from usual.

However. "Can't we do something about Claes being tied up every night?"

"Mr. Loren, are you suggesting we release a wolf upon a flock of sheep?"

Their traveling companions were all young women—and each beautiful enough to warrant Lapis's caution. Loren huffed a sigh as he looked at the one-person tent Claes was bound and shoved into whenever he wasn't on lookout duty.

On the upside, their meals were far better than those of any previous quest. They were using their own supplies, not laying a finger on Rose's convoy, but Lapis had purchased groceries incomparable to their previous preserved rations. This, in turn, made the women of Claes's party even more critical toward the man, not that Lapis seemed to mind.

"It turns out even the quality of dried meat greatly differs if you put in a bit of money," Lapis noted.

"Just how much did you spend on this?" Loren asked.

"That's a secret. Anyway, as far as I'm concerned, I didn't spend a thing. Would you like some wine? It isn't even diluted like our usual fare. This is vintage stuff, Mr. Loren."

"What are you doing? No, don't get me wrong. I'll have some."

He knew he shouldn't drink on the job, but he wasn't about to waste Lapis's effort to bring such a rare treat.

"We bought bread without any cheap filler in the flour, and the cheese is the nice kind, so if we hold it over the fire for a second... Perfect. That should go wonderfully with the wine."

"You're eating your fill..."

"Then add a bit of sliced meat as an accent. Unfortunately, we can't do anything about vegetables. They go bad over long trips."

"Didn't I see you shoving some potatoes into the bonfire?"

"I'll dig them out later and spread butter over them. They're delicious, you know? Won't you have some?"

"I'll take one. But you know..."

Rose and her villagers prepared a hearty stew in their cooking pot, so they were eating decently. However, Claes's party was washing down hard brown bread and tough, leathery dried meat with thinned wine or plain water. Lapis had no reservations about feasting right beside them, which drastically lowered their morale.

Loren had considered sharing if they had any to spare, but Lapis had prioritized quality over quantity. Their fellow party's plight couldn't compel him to give up his own share, so he reluctantly partook in the opportunity for an extravagant meal.

And so the caravan went on. On the third day, however, the atmosphere shifted just so. They had at last veered off the highway onto a side path that would bring them to the village. Roads leading to small settlements hardly saw any traffic. These paths were mostly used to deliver supplies, as they were attempting to do, or they were taken by traveling merchants who went from village to village. It was hard to say that they were properly maintained.

The carts clattered and shook, and the party's pace dropped. What's more, there were no soldiers to guard the paths, which meant an inevitable decline in public order. Here was the stretch that Rose had hired guards for.

"This might be a harder job than expected," Lapis mused as she looked around.

Loren examined one of the wagons, which had its wheel caught in a pothole. The villagers might have been able to manage the route with empty wagons, but now the vehicles were so loaded down that they could barely move under their own weight. It became a Herculean task to lift them out of simple cavities.

"This is about par for the course," Loren told her. "It's the same wherever you go."

Loren casually lifted the wagon with one hand. At the same time, a villager spurred on the donkey pulling the cart, freeing it from the rut. Loren dusted off his hands and watched the group for a few seconds before ambling after. Like Lapis, he took a good look around.

They were moving across an empty plain of grass. Visibility was good, but that was also true for anyone or anything that might be watching them. There wasn't anywhere to run or hide, and Loren felt a hint of unease.

"We'll know in an instant if something comes after us, but we don't have any defenses."

"That is why we hired adventurers to guard us," Rose said in reply to Loren's murmur.

Her charming voice made Claes weak in the knees. But he steeled his expression under the harsh eyes of his party and offered something like a half scold, half complaint to Rose. "If it's that dangerous, you ought to offer a higher payout! What if no one had accepted?"

Rose just smiled back at him. "But just look at how many fine adventurers answered my call yet again."

Loren snorted and ended the conversation there. That was as good as admitting that she always posted her guard request with the same provisions. He was impressed that she had always managed to rope in the help she needed, but that mystery quickly resolved itself.

Rose leaned in close and whispered, "I might need help again. If that happens, I'll be counting on your good services."

Her gestures and voice made her tactics clear; Rose depended on adventurers like Claes falling for her wiles. Loren didn't know just how far she went to secure her contracts, but he imagined her to be quite the determined one. He needed to distance himself from her without making it a whole scene.

"It was just a whim this time," he said. "There won't be another—not for us, at least."

"Oh, my, you're quite cold." Rose subtly bent over, folding her arms to emphasize her chest.

Loren waved his hand, urging her to go away as if he were driving off an annoying insect. Claes kept his eyes screwed shut.

Loren didn't have anything against someone using what they were given, but it was wearisome to be the target of something so blatant.

Claes's party muttered darkly amongst themselves.

"If our leader had even half of his self-restraint..."

"That's a waste to even think about."

"This must be one of god's trials."

Lapis looked rather triumphant, for whatever reason; that nagged at him, but Loren returned his attention to their surroundings as soon as Rose left him alone.

He picked up a scent on the next breeze, a smell that one never expected to detect on the plains. He glanced upwind.

When planning an attack, it was incredibly ill-advised to come from upwind, but a bit of tailwind wasn't so bad if stealth offered no particular advantage.

"Something's here!" Loren called out, and the air immediately grew tense.

The smell on the wind was one of sour body odor and leather. The scent of danger—one Loren had grown accustomed to after living on the battlefield.

"Bandits, eh?" Claes swiftly unsheathed his longsword.

Their foes, who had concealed themselves amongst the long grass, rose one after another from the grass surrounding the caravan.

Their equipment had given them away—rancid leather armor in terrible condition. Their weapons varied wildly, and no two seemed the same. The bandits had hidden themselves a short distance away. No doubt they would have preferred more time before their dramatic reveal, but Loren had beaten them to the punch.

Even with that advantage, Loren immediately knew it would be impossible to run away. Rose and her people might be able to flee if they left the wagons behind, but it would be hard to convince them to cast aside their village's lifeline. Sure, survival in the moment came first. But if the bandits stole their supplies, then the villagers would no longer be able to sustain themselves, and all that would await them was an even crueler end.

Even so, Loren posed the question to Rose. "Do you feel like abandoning these wagons and making a break for it?"

"W-we can't do that! Without these supplies, we're..."

Exactly the response he'd expected. There was little choice in the matter. Loren scratched his head; if they couldn't run, they would have to intercept.

He focused his eyes, picking out how many bandits were coming at them—roughly twenty armed men.

"Couldn't you handle that on your own?" he muttered to Lapis, almost despite himself.

Lapis immediately drove an elbow into his flank. To an outsider, it might look as though Lapis had retaliated against an unreasonable request. However, Lapis was a demon, and Loren felt a chill shoot down his spine as her elbow dug into him.

"What are you talking about, Mr. Loren? I am but a simple priest. I know how to fight a bit for self-defense, but there's no possible way I could take on so many bandits."

Loren hadn't taken too much damage from the blow. The hit against his armor sounded worse than it was, and really, she'd just poked him, more or less. He looked at her, wondering if she'd restrained herself, only to see she seemed terribly irritated. Apparently, his new gear had protected him from her full wrath.

Then he remembered that with Claes's party and Rose's villagers watching, he couldn't rely on Lapis's physical abilities.

"Sorry, that was in bad taste," he apologized, pitching his voice to be heard by the others.

Lapis nodded, her expression softening. "As long as you understand."

While Lapis and Loren bickered, Claes stepped forward. "Then I'll take care of them. Those numbers are no match for me."

One of his party members, the knight Leila, matched his readied blade. "I'd rather not kill anyone, but it is my duty to protect the weak."

Ange took a stance with her staff to support them, while the priest Laure watched over the situation from even farther back.

"All right, then we'll look out for any detached forces and protect the cargo," said Loren.

"That sounds easy enough..." said Lapis. "Ahem, I mean: We need to ensure the safety of the villagers too."

We can leave this one to Claes, Loren thought as he reached for the sword on his back and positioned himself between the bandits and the wagons. Lapis scampered behind him with a hand over her mouth—she had to take care not to misspeak again.

Just because weapons were drawn, that didn't mean everyone jumped right to the slicing and dicing. It sure seemed like the rough-looking armed men and their stink had been waiting around to ambush them, but that didn't guarantee they were bandits.

Loren didn't mind cutting them down without another word, but Claes insisted on posing the question.

"Who are you lot?! Identify yourselves!" he called out.

He received no answer.

The presumed-bandits each readied their own weapons, spreading out to cut off any escape before charging en masse. Only two fighters—Claes and Leila—had stepped out to intercept them, and the bandits must have thought that twenty men would be unstoppable.

"Do we have to put in a bit of work, then?" Loren asked.

"I'm not so sure," Lapis replied, nonchalant.

And with one backward glance at them, Claes took off. Loren's eyes widened ever so slightly at Claes's speed. He had seen Claes fight and use his abilities a few times before. He knew something of the man's pace and power, but with this charge, Claes smashed his own record.

"He's faster than before."

Two fighters couldn't hold back twenty foes. That was impossible even for Loren. If the fight moved close to the villagers or the wagons, he would have to steel himself to see some damage. The only way to prevent this would be to fight a good distance from their convoy—meaning to rush out. And to pray and hope that their client never made contact with the enemy.

"But still, a few will slip past him."

Surely she hadn't heard him, but a beat after Claes, Leila raced out with her blonde hair billowing behind her.

"Kill the men! Restrain the women! This is where we earn our bread! Put your back into it, men!" cried a voice among the bandits.

When Loren heard those orders, he was about to draw his sword, but he stopped. Lapis tilted her head, trying to infer his reasons, sure he had them.

"If we were running out there, I'd draw," he said. "But if I fight with this thing here, I'll ruin the supplies with the splatter."

The force behind Loren's swings could split a human body in two without any resistance. This was fundamentally not a bad thing, but Rose's supplies contained clothes and food; it would be a pity to stain all that with human remains.

"Okay, then let's hope that Mr. Claes defeats them all," Lapis said with an understanding nod.

I don't see that happening, thought Loren as he watched Claes make contact with the enemy vanguard.

Claes's first mark relied on brute force, swinging a decently thick axe. Any attempt to parry with a sword would doubtless break the latter, but Claes caught the blow head-on with his blade. The shrill grating of metal resounded from the meeting of axe and sword, and while the axe should have won out, it was instead repelled.

The impact wasn't strong enough to drive the axe out of the man's hands, but his stance crumbled. Despite his best attempts to pull his axe back, Claes's movements were several times too fast for him to keep up with.

It ended with a single line through his throat. Not a slash, but a thrust. Claes drew his blade back just as fast as he had unleashed it and took a step toward his next mark.

He sewed his way through brandished blades, his own sword slashing left and right. Then two bandits fell, spraying blood from the deep gashes in the sides of their necks. Claes was gone even before the blood splatter could stain him. He flicked off the meager liquid coating his blade and turned toward the rest of his foes.

Taking this all in, the bandits froze.

"They're losing their nerve, those idiots," Loren muttered. The bandits were reacting poorly. Their only option now was to forsake their allies and slip past Claes to attack Rose directly.

In the time it would take Claes to slay one or two of them, they would be able to kill or injure the villagers—and perhaps the threat to innocents would throw Claes off his game. That was their only chance to win.

Yet seeing their allies slain so easily, they faltered. They froze up and were unable to even summon bravado.

"Though that makes our job a whole lot easier."

Any bandits who slipped through Claes would have become Loren's responsibility, but the odds of that happenstance were falling drastically. As long as the bandits didn't approach the supplies, he saw no reason to rush out; he could entrust this to Claes and Leila.

While Loren thought the matter over, Claes killed another two, and Leila slew her first after a late start. Her speed wasn't on the same level as Claes's, but she was quite adept with her blade. She had an orthodox style, but her technique was backed both by training and real combat experience.

A bandit who made light of a woman's sword and approached with a laugh was easily sliced in twain, and only then did his compatriots finally understand that they were no match for the adventurers they had challenged.

"Why are there two master swordsmen all the way out here?!" the leader of the bandits cried out.

Loren understood where he was coming from. No run-of-the-mill bandit assumed that they would stumble across the holder of a rare gift and the knight who served him. If these ne'er-do-wells had assumed they were just picking a fight with some mediocre adventurers, then the attempt to win with overwhelming numbers hadn't been utterly foolish.

"Unfortunately, you chose the wrong caravan to mess with."

"Don't think you're getting away! If I let guys like you run free, you'll grow in number and go after other travelers. I'll cut you down here."

"Dammit! I'm not going down here! Run!"

It was impossible to expect an army's level of coordination and morale from a gang of bandits. They had already lost close to half their number to Claes and Leila, and the fear that they might be stabbed next had destroyed any lingering enthusiasm. And once morale collapsed, it was all downhill from there.

The bandits cast down their weapons, turned, and tried to flee. Claes hesitated for a moment upon seeing them turn tail. He seemed to contemplate whether it was all right to stab a defenseless and defeated enemy in the back.

This kind of thought came to Claes naturally, and as a knight, Leila had been taught chivalry. As far as Loren was concerned, they were both incredibly naïve.

Even if you meant to spare your foe, it was unthinkable to let worthless bandits get away just because they'd exposed their cowardly backs. Loren would have chased them down. But a part of him understood why that was difficult, and he decided to be satisfied with the fact that the supplies were safe.

However, someone else didn't think so, and she immediately acted against the fleeing bandits.

"May scattered sand shut their eyes!" Ange chanted as she held out her staff. "*Sleep*."

This magic—a spell that immediately plunged its targets into deep slumber—took effect. Their leader was the first to fall. Then, one by one, those around him were afflicted and collapsed on the spot. The remaining bandits instinctively stopped as they saw their comrades topple over. These stragglers were met by Claes and Leila, who had ultimately given chase. In no time at all, the bandits were either dead or put to sleep and bound.

"I expected more from those numbers," said Lapis.

"There wasn't any place for us to step in," Loren replied.

As Claes and Leila returned with their blades sheathed, shrill cheers erupted from the villagers. Rose immediately raced over to Claes and jumped into his embrace. As Claes caught her, the cheers grew even more fevered, though his party members did not look amused.

"You're as masterful as I thought, Claes," said Rose.

"No, the enemy was simply weak—and I'm not the only one who fought."

"Perhaps, but I must start by thanking *you*. I was honestly worried about what might happen, but I'm glad you're all right."

Rose had wrapped an arm around Claes's waist, and as he

held her tight, the soft twin peaks between the two of them were smushed into strange new shapes. The pressure must have reached Claes even through his leather armor. He inevitably broke into a broad grin. While Ange and the rest of his party stared daggers into him, he was so entranced by Rose that he didn't even notice.

I'm surprised they can operate as a party like this, Loren mused as he wandered over to the bound, sleeping bandits.

"Are you going to investigate?" Lapis asked.

Loren stooped down beside the bandits and began looking over their armor and the weapons they'd dropped. "There's a war going on, right? I thought they might be deserters or something."

"Weren't they a little too weak to be deserters?"

At least it looked that way to Lapis. As far as Loren could tell, the bandits hadn't been that bad. It was just that Claes was far stronger. The bandits wouldn't have frozen up if Claes hadn't exhibited so much strength. If they'd continued their charge, they probably would have caused quite a bit of damage to the supplies or villagers.

"Anyway, looks like that's not the case. I know it sounds strange to call them honest, but they're honest-to-goodness bandits."

Loren could tell they weren't fallen mercenaries either. Anyone who had experienced a few battlefields wouldn't have gone possum like that.

"Hey, you! How long are you going to cling to Claes?!"

"Th-that's obscene!"

"And you too, Claes! Do something about that lewd look on your face!"

"Umm, Mr. Loren? What are we going to do about the survivors?" Lapis asked.

"Well, it would be a pain if they have comrades to call on. We can't bring them with us, so we'll finish them off here."

Ange pulled Claes away from Rose. Laure showered him with criticism while Leila greeted his face with an iron fist.

Claes went flying before he could get a word in. As Rose looked on in horror, Leila grabbed Claes by the collar and dragged him off. Though Rose tried to chase after him, she was stopped by intimidating looks from Ange and Laure. Loren pulled out the knife he usually used to butcher prey and approached the bandits who dreamt sweetly, unaware of their incoming fate.

"Oh, hey, Loren. What happened to the bandits?"

"Don't worry about it. They'll survive with some luck, and otherwise, someone else will finish them off."

Even though Claes had just endured punishment from his party members, he was bursting with energy. Ange was no more than a magician, but she certainly knew where to aim; either Claes had gotten sturdier, or her attacks were so commonplace they no longer bothered him.

However, it was strange to think that Dame Leila's punch had so little effect. Even more so that Claes had survived his priest's attacks unharmed... Or so Loren thought, until he realized a normal priest couldn't punch hard enough to knock a swordsman unconscious. He tilted his head, wondering exactly when that possibility had lodged itself so firmly in his head.

"More importantly, aren't you stronger than the last time I saw you?" he asked Claes.

"Of course I am. Despite everything, I've got a lot of hopes pinned on me, and the backing of a country too." Claes blurted that out pretty casually, though Loren was certain he shouldn't be privy to government dealings.

Was it really all right to tell me that? he wondered. But surely Claes knew what he was doing. "By country, do you mean..."

"Well, obviously Waargenberg. What else would it be?"

Loren didn't know what he would have done if Claes had named some other place. He let out a relieved sigh. It would have been a huge headache if an adventurer supported by some other nation was operating in Waargenberg. Although there were surely adventurers like that out there somewhere.

It was exceedingly difficult to send knights and soldiers into foreign lands, but relatively easy to dispatch adventurers and mercenaries. As a matter of fact, Loren knew of mercenary companies that were specifically hired by nations to perform acts of subterfuge.

Of course, he wasn't going to spread that information around. It was a trade secret.

If all went well, those companies could continue operating with national backing, but once the information got out, the country backing them would play dumb. Meanwhile, the nation that discovered the ruse would use any means at their disposal to crush the company. It all made for a risky business endeavor.

The same could be said for adventurers. There were adventurers who did the work of spies, but unsurprisingly, Claes wasn't one of them.

"We've been through a bit together, you and I," Claes said. "I don't think Leila will be too angry that I let that slip."

"If you're going to spread information like that, you should really check with her first."

The kingdom probably wanted Leila to keep a keen eye on Claes and his big mouth. Loren swore to himself that he would never tell Claes any secrets.

In any case, the party pressed on. A night later, before noon on the fourth day, they arrived at their destination. Apart from the bandit attack, nothing of note happened. No monster attacks, and no second helping of outlaws. The road was steady, and Loren nurtured a faint hope that finally, he had roped an easy job.

These hopes slowly fell apart as he laid eyes on the village and the residents who flocked out to greet them.

"This village is definitely strange, Mr. Loren."

There were cheers as Rose and her helpers immediately got to work unloading their cargo. But Lapis was right, the scenery was certainly strange.

There wasn't a single man among the villagers who came to greet them. Not only that, the villagers were entirely composed of old women and children; he could only make out two people who could be called maidens.

"It's not just that this village has no men. It hardly has any working-age people at all."

"How's a village like that supposed to function...? At least, that's what I'd like to ask, but I can't deny it when it's right before my eyes."

Rose's settlement was supposed to be a farming village. There were fields spread all around, and they made their livelihood by raising produce. The fact that they had no male labor on hand was beyond strange—it was abnormal. With so many small children and elderly, it was hard to think they could sustain themselves.

It seemed Claes picked up on this abnormality as well. He had a stiff expression on his face as he approached Loren. "Have you noticed, Loren?"

"Yeah, I'm pretty sure anyone would've noticed."

"Is this supposed to be heaven?"

For a moment, he couldn't understand what Claes was saying. Loren closely observed the man's face. He was unable to pick out any humor in Claes's expression—he was serious. Loren slowly clenched his fist.

"Wait, wait! A punch from you will snap my neck!"

"Don't worry, I'll just rearrange your facial structure a bit is all."

"That's even worse!"

"Now look here..."

The kid hardly put up a defense, but Loren gave up on hitting him. He loosened his fist, grabbed Claes by the shoulder, turned him toward the crowd of villagers as he whispered into his ear.

"You don't feel anything off, looking at that?"

"It's all women. What a truly wonderful village they have here."

"Notice anything else...?" Loren stifled his irritation but tightened his grip.

As Claes grimaced in pain, he desperately searched for the answer Loren sought. Eventually, he concluded, "Th-the fact that there are a lot of little girls and older women? But Loren, it's not nice to discriminate against women based on their age and—it's going to snap! It's really going to snap!"

"Are you completely indiscriminate?"

"How rude! I simply don't judge women based on those factors!" Claes declared, conviction strong.

This was almost refreshing, in a sense, and Loren released his shoulder. As Claes reached a hand around to rub his aching bones, he finally tilted his head.

"But it really is curious that there aren't any men around."

"There's actually a reason for that," Rose interrupted.

Loren had been so preoccupied with Claes that he hadn't noticed her approaching; her sudden arrival made him reel back a few steps.

Claes, on the other hand, was completely unmoved. He smiled to relieve Rose's concern. "What sort of reason is it, Chief? I would love to hear it."

"Oh, Claes... But what do you intend to do once you have?"

"That goes without saying. If there's a woman in trouble, I simply have to help her out. If there's anything I can do, I will."

"Oh, *Claes*," Rose moaned, overcome with emotion.

Meanwhile, Loren tried to slip away quietly. Even if he heard about the village's predicament, he could hardly dash off to set it to rights. Only the protagonists of fairy tales could act so foolishly. As far as Loren was concerned, this was no place for an adventurer or a mercenary.

Perhaps it was precisely because of Claes's generous nature that he was considered a boon to his nation, but Loren had no obligation to tag along with his antics.

Unfortunately, Claes reached out and grabbed him by his belt without even looking, still smiling with his eyes locked onto Rose. "Where are you trying to go, Loren? Hear out the chief's story with me."

"I decline. I ain't interested."

"We'll listen even if you aren't interested. I *am* the leader of this party, you know."

What's he on about? Loren was about to retort. But come to think of it, though temporarily, they were indeed registered as members of Claes's party, and Claes was indeed the leader. He could ignore Claes, for sure, but it was an unwritten rule to follow the leader on the job. Ever the faithful man, Loren couldn't just throw his scruples away because he didn't want to sit through this tale of woe.

"Just so you know, if you take her job offer, that's a separate fee," he said. "Also, even if I do hear it out, there's no guarantee I'll join you. I have to discuss that with Lapis first. That good with you?"

This was a deviation from the job, Loren insisted. They would require a separate fee to cover for their participation.

Claes continued to smile as he whispered, "I get you. No matter what happens, I'm not going to ask you to work for free."

"Good grief, can't we just do the job we were hired for...?"

Loren just didn't understand why anyone would voluntarily stick their heads into trouble. However, once he looked at Claes again—and at Rose—the reason became clear enough.

"To tell you the truth, there is another village a little ways north of us..."

"Is there something wrong with that village? Are you at war with them?"

"No, we've had friendly relations up until now. Many people would come and go between our villages. But the other day, people simply stopped coming back."

Normally, people made the trip between the villages daily, yet travel had suddenly come to a complete halt. Out of concern, Rose had sent several of the village's young men to see what was going on, but they had never returned.

"I knew something had to be afoot, so I sent more men the second time. I begged the soldiers protecting the village to accompany them..."

"And the second group didn't come back either?"

Rose nodded.

It wasn't so strange for communication with a small village to suddenly fall apart. Perhaps there had been a monster attack or a bandit raid. Perhaps they had been dragged into the nearby war. When all was said and done, farming villages went under easily. New settlements were especially susceptible to ending in such ways, as the likelihood of monster and bandit attacks was several times higher for them than it was for places that had long since been settled. These unfortunate incidents were nothing to write home about.

"After no one returned from the second search party, I told the villagers to forget about our neighbors and warned them not to get close."

Rose's decision had come, perhaps, a little too late, but acting late was better than acting never. She wrote a petition to the kingdom to request aid in investigating the abnormality and she fully intended to send it. However, even as she penned her letter, she'd noticed her villagers wandering in the direction of the neighboring settlement in the dead of the night.

"Is that why the men are all gone?"

"It was only men at first. Along the way, it started happening to the women as well. Something seems to be drawing them."

If it were just the men, Loren would have suspected a succubus. With both men and women, he couldn't be so sure. The reason almost certainly lay in the neighboring village, but as no one had returned, there was little information to be gleaned.

"Claes, if you can find it in your heart to help our village, I beg of you—won't you venture to the neighboring settlement and either find what is happening or save our villagers who have disappeared?"

"Right, let's see. I need to talk it over with my comrades, so I can't give you an immediate answer. But rest assured, I'm not the sort of man who can abandon a woman in need."

"I see... You have my gratitude, Claes..."

Claes smiled to reassure Rose, and she swooned into his arms. As Loren watched Claes embrace her back, he wondered just how many future problems would be avoided if Ange just up and stabbed the man.

3 Unification to Arrival

"IF THEY'RE REALLY in this much trouble, then we have a duty to lend a hand."

To Loren's surprise, Leila was the first one to throw her support behind Claes.

Unloading the wagons wasn't in their job description, so while the villagers toiled, the party gathered in a room in Rose's house and held a meeting. The topic, naturally, was the strange events happening in the village, and whether or not they would accept Rose's request to investigate.

Loren had truly thought that Claes would be in the lone voice in support, yet Leila proved otherwise.

"I may be an adventurer for now, but as you may have guessed from my armor, I'm also a knight," she said. "I am unable to overlook a cry for help from those in need."

"That's the spirit, Leila. I knew you'd understand."

"Although the sordid tale of our leader getting tangled up in this *is* irritating..." Leila's clenched fist shook, though Claes didn't seem to notice. He simply held out his open palm for a friendly handshake. Leila gritted her teeth, but as far as Loren could tell, it was impossible to teach Claes a lesson without the use of extreme force.

"As a priest, err, I...also can't ignore those in trouble..." Laure timidly aligned herself with Leila.

Now that the first vote had been cast, Loren wasn't shocked by Laure's support. Those who served the gods were duty-bound to help the needy regardless of financial benefit. It would be quite peculiar if a priest acted as though the troubles of the people were none of their business.

"As a priest of the god of knowledge, I also think it is wrong to ignore those in need," Lapis conceded sulkily. Though she tried to keep a poker face, her eyes looked dead, and her level voice rang hollow. For what it was worth, Loren had expected this as well.

Had Loren been her only travel companion, she would have immediately advised against sticking out their necks without a promised reward. Even if she was only paying it lip service, she had to keep up the charade of a good-natured priest.

That left only Loren and Ange. The odds that Ange would go against the group were incredibly low. She would have to be quite the contrarian, and it was hard to imagine someone with that much backbone tagging after Claes for so long.

"There...doesn't seem to be much point in me voting against it," she said. "I'll agree, but you'll owe me one. Is that good with you, Claes?"

"Thank you, Ange."

With two of her party members on board, it would be a poor move to go against them and sour Claes's impression of her. Ange had acted in a kind of self-interest. When she stuck out a pinky finger to seal the deal, Claes looped his around it with a smile.

Ange's face turned red, and she probably counted herself satisfied. Loren looked at her coldly, resolving to speak his mind, even without an ally. "I'm not doing it for free. That's the one thing I won't budge on."

If he couldn't get out of this, then he needed to negotiate the best deal possible. At the very least, he would have expected bonus payment on a normal job, but even the odds of that seemed slim.

After all, the village chief Rose had seduced Claes into the initial work—she didn't look like she was about to shell out any extra coin. She didn't seem cruel enough to send them off with no reward either, but worst-case scenario, Claes was the only one who would end up with "payment."

Shaking Claes down for the fee would also prove difficult. Claes had already paid them fifty silver, and his wallet was light. He was receiving support from a nation, but that didn't mean he received unlimited unconditional financial freedom. There was a limit to his budget.

"You have a point," Leila said with a nod. "We may be in the same party, but it doesn't make sense to force a temporary member to bend to our whims."

This was said specifically to Loren—Lapis had already agreed to take part and was in no position to demand a reward. Lapis kept a strained smile on her face, a powerless laugh escaping her lips.

"Then how about this?" said Leila. "Claes and the four of us who agreed to join him will pay two silver each. Would ten silver be enough to hire you?"

She proposed the plan as if it were a work of genius, and the air around Lapis grew even heavier. Claes's party didn't seem to notice. While Loren could tell Lapis was livid, it would be strange for him to suddenly declare he didn't need a reward after all. And given her own position, Lapis couldn't possibly say she didn't want to pay her share.

"That'll have to do." And so, Loren immediately agreed to Leila's terms.

Perhaps he could have bartered for greater payment. After all, no one was certain how difficult the quest would be, and keeping Loren with them might make all the difference. Surely there would have been more in it for him if he'd pushed.

But at the same time, that would've meant squeezing money out of Lapis and harming his own partner.

"You have my gratitude, Loren." Leila bowed her head, but Loren stopped her.

"We're all in the same boat," he muttered. "Not like I could return to Kaffa alone."

"Now that that's decided, let's head right over to that neighboring village!" Claes proclaimed with a broad grin, only to be smacked by Leila and Ange. Laure just smiled, but she did step on Claes's fallen figure.

Lapis still had that same sickly smile plastered on her face, and Loren leaned close. "I'll return that two silver later," he whispered.

"It's money I've spent. I'm not expecting it back..." she replied, her expression not moving in the slightest.

"No need to be stubborn about it," Loren said with a frown.

"Then treat me to something worth two silver once the job is over. That should settle it." Lapis's expression finally changed. She looked at him tiredly, and Loren nodded.

If that was enough to get her back in a good mood, it was a cheap buy.

Upon seeing Loren's response, Lapis sandwiched her face between her hands and massaged it back into her usual expression.

"N-now...about that neighboring village..." Claes said, attempting to take the lead. He was promptly ignored. Everyone headed straight to Rose to secure as much support from the village as possible.

"First, we need to get directions and information from that hag, as well as food supplies to sustain ourselves."

"It would be nice if she offered some reward, but I doubt she intends to since Claes already accepted... How loathsome..."

"Why does he have to fall for these things so easily? Seriously..."

"I'll have to take this as one of my god's trials..."

"Then that's quite a mean-spirited god you have there, Ms. Laure. Not that I can say much, now that I've been roped into it."

Rose's response was as they'd expected: "Our village does not have much to give... If the country's leadership would only take care of things, I wouldn't have needed to make the request."

It was even worse how she kept glancing at Leila, dressed in the kingdom's armor.

Rose had only written a letter, and she'd never actually mailed the thing. To be fair, Loren understood her doubt that anyone would answer one backwater village chief's call for help. The nation was at war. They would hardly go out of their way to resolve a problem plaguing an insignificant farming settlement.

As she was also well aware of this, Leila only averted her eyes.

"And Claes has already most graciously accepted," Rose continued with a smile.

Claes chuckled bashfully, and as Ange and Laure immediately thrust their fists into his abdomen, Loren spoke to Rose in a tired voice.

"Can't say I don't know where you're coming from. But aren't you goin' about it a bit dirty?"

"Please don't make me sound like the villain here. Those who do not have the skills to fight must rely on the compassion of adventurers."

"Yeah, I get that. But it ain't nice to shove it all on us without putting any of your own skin in the game."

Loren could understand that the weak and the lowly needed help from the strong. Even so, he believed that those seeking help needed to shoulder some of the burdens as well. These notions were merely waved off with a smile—Rose didn't even attempt to respond.

What now? he wondered. He lowered his voice to a whisper. "Then the village ain't gonna help us in any way?" he asked Rose.

"It would be more accurate to say we couldn't even if we wanted to."

"I see. Then there are no two ways about it. Incidentally, the fact that there's no reward naturally means it doesn't matter if we fail, and we don't have any obligation to report back, right?"

For a moment, it seemed she didn't take his meaning. Her face turned dubious, then grim as Loren continued.

"So long as there's a reward, we shoulder a bit of risk upon failure, and whether things go well or not, we need to tell you what's up. No reward means we don't have to do any of that."

"You mean..."

"I mean, the moment we set off, we can just say we failed and return to Kaffa, end of story."

No reward meant they lost absolutely nothing by failing. They could suborn Claes the moment they left the village, declare they had botched the quest, and return to Kaffa. Given Leila's knightly disposition, that plan likely wouldn't fly, but Rose couldn't be certain of their circumstances or character.

"You'd put us in such a bind! Just an awful bind!"

"Then help out a bit, would you? You're making it sound like it's only natural you'd be saved, just because you're weak. Though our leader's womanizing is the real problem here."

"H-however..."

"I'm not telling you to fork over cash. It can be food or water—or ale—there's just got to be something. You could lend us a donkey to carry supplies. I'm telling you to show you're at least trying to support us."

Loren understood that the village didn't have much to spare. With the bulk of its workforce missing, the village had to be struggling to farm for their own subsistence; with such an uncertain future, it was prudent to preserve their stockpile as much as possible.

Still, there was nothing to admire in asking others to resolve the village's issues without shouldering any of the risks, and though Rose broke into a cold sweat at Loren's demand, she desperately started running the numbers in her head.

In the end, Loren secured some food, medical supplies, and a donkey to carry them. He had negotiated by dangling drastic terms in front of Rose's face. The quest wasn't mediated through the guild—it was issued to them directly, so turning tail wouldn't leave a stain on their record. Even if someone at the guild caught wind of it, it would only give Claes a black mark as party leader.

Rose looked incredibly reluctant, but Loren had to wonder how much of it was an act. She was hiring six iron rank adventurers, who usually came with a price tag of dozens of silver. With that in mind, the supplies she offered in the name of support were incredibly cheap.

"We could have gotten more if we negotiated a bit," Lapis whispered, sounding rather disappointed. Outwardly, Lapis supported Claes's position, and thus couldn't complain too loudly.

"She might do something to spite us if we take too much. We should act in moderation," Loren said.

He knew all too well that nothing good came of getting greedy. He'd managed to scrounge up some supplies from nothing and so convinced himself to be satisfied with the result.

According to Rose's explanation, the neighboring village was about a stound away by foot. The villagers were busy sorting through the supplies brought from Kaffa, but Loren and the rest of the adventurers had nothing better to do. They promptly set off.

"Not that I want to go," Loren grumbled.

"I understand how you feel, but isn't it about time you gave up?" Leila responded with a wry smile.

However, what bothered Loren wasn't what she assumed. He needed to correct her. "I've given up on the bonus payment. We got some supplies, and I'm being paid separately. I'm not ecstatic, but I've accepted that."

"Then what are you so bothered about?"

"The location of this other village."

According to Rose, the nearest village was positioned to the north. It was only about as big as Rose's village, but there was a rather large forest beyond it. From what Loren could tell from looking at the map, the battlefield of the war was just past those woods.

"It gets more dangerous the closer we are to the battlefield. You can understand why I'm not delighted, right?"

As a former mercenary, the battlefield was one of his old haunts. But that didn't mean he was leaping at the chance to return; he knew the danger better than anyone.

"It's a forest away, and that forest is pretty vast. Is there really any need to worry?" said Laure, who seemed to be tracing the map in her head.

Loren scratched his head as he answered. "If they're clashing head-on, then sure. But if someone gets the bright idea to circumnavigate the battlefield to flank the enemy, then their cavalry could easily take a detour through a forest or two."

Soldiers on horseback could be quite terrifying. Their mobility and charging force were so formidable that foot soldiers had little hope of matching them. Loren didn't want to make any fun new cavalry friends.

"You're quite the worrywart," said Ange. She sounded surprised.

Loren shrugged. "You've got to worry at least this much, or you'll never survive. That's the sort of place the battlefield is."

"Then I definitely don't want to get near it."

"As long as you're adventuring with that guy, you might be forced to go whether you like it or not." Loren tipped his chin toward Claes, who was leading the donkey at the front. "Claes is backed by a government, right? He might be sent out one of these days."

Ange had a pensive look on her face. "We're doing our best to make sure it doesn't come to that, but you can never be too sure."

The nation took in skilled adventurers partly for their combat prowess, but they were mostly expected to discover and search ancient ruins or exterminate dangerous monsters. In that way, they had a utility that far exceeded their use in battle, and everyone understood how foolish it would be to send them to a place where fighting was all they could do. But a kingdom with its back against the wall might see no other option.

"Lately, I've gotten to wondering if I should find a new party," said Ange.

"That's none of my business... But seriously, I'm more curious as to why you haven't left yet."

Claes wasn't a bad person, or at least Loren didn't think he was. He could at times be a little arrogant, but he was generally virtuous. He was a philanderer, but that largely manifested in a strange chivalry and a willingness to help out no matter the cost. Some might have said this made him the ultimate philanthropist.

"He has the disposition of a hero from a fairy tale," said Lapis. Her evaluation of Claes was accepted by everyone in the conversation. The only one who was left out of it was Claes, who looked over his shoulder, a miserable frown on his face.

"Can you please not talk about me behind my back?"

"Just think of it as a valuable chance to hear your comrades' frank thoughts about you," Loren told him up-front.

Claes sighed, looked ahead again, and continued leading the donkey along.

Loren snorted as he watched the man's back, then nearly choked at Ange's next words.

"By the way, Lapis. What do you think about Loren?"

"What do you mean by that?" Lapis asked back. She maintained perfect calm at this sudden query.

Ange's eyes were brimming with interest as she tugged on Lapis's sleeve. "You're asking what we think about Claes, so isn't it your turn to say what you think about Loren?"

"I fail to see the connection."

"I'm interested in that too," Leila joined in, and Laure was nodding beside her. "Oh, it's nothing too deep. Just think of it as an inoffensive conversation to have along the way."

The topic had taken a strange turn. Though Loren cupped a hand to his mouth, Lapis still seemed completely unmoved. She placed an index finger on her cheek and thought a moment before answering with a smile.

"I want to invite him to my hometown soon."

"What? You mean you want to introduce him to your parents?" Leila said, startled. Despite Ange and Laure's reddened faces, for some reason, they seemed delighted to hear that.

Lapis calmly went on, "But I am a priest, you see. To be perfectly honest, I find it difficult to take the next step."

Priests weren't prohibited from marriage. However, they served as representatives of gods, and having too many failed relationships could potentially reflect poorly on their god's reputation. Thus, priests were generally quite cautious when choosing partners.

That was how the other women interpreted Lapis's words, at least. She was fine with introducing Loren to her parents, but she had yet to decide if she wanted a lifelong commitment. What a charming expression of modesty from an extremely holy woman!

"I'm glad to hear you're getting along, Loren," said Claes.

"Shut it. Keep walking."

Claes grinned at him, and Loren delivered a swift kick to his behind. He thought he had pulled his punch, so to speak, but Claes stumbled as his feet were lifted off the ground.

Realizing that Loren had failed to control himself, Claes rubbed his aching bottom and reminded himself to use *Boost* to raise his defense the next time he teased Loren, lest he emerge from chummy male bonding with a major injury.

"Still, I guess you priests have it rough," Ange said, eyeing Loren and Claes's antics with old exhaustion.

"Err, Ange," Laure timidly chimed in. "I'm a priest too..."

"That goes for you, too, then. If you like Claes, then be resolute about it. He's not the sort of guy who will be content with just one romantic partner."

"Err, umm..."

"He'll definitely have mistresses and lovers. I've already steeled myself for that," Leila declared, chest puffed out bravely. Everyone apart from Claes wondered just what she was so proud of, but the man in question didn't seem to mind the stares he received.

"You really need to do something about your personality," Loren told him. "Weren't you gunning for Ange?"

A while back, Loren had been present when Ange had quite nearly died. Claes's concern for her back then hadn't seemed false. And yet Claes was so easily wooed by other women... Loren didn't understand him at all. In fact, it irritated him to the point that it made him consider getting in another kick.

Escaping to a safe distance, Claes confidently nodded.

"Naturally, Ange is the one I love most in the world. I would never lie about that."

"In that case..."

"But to offer my love equally to Leila and Laure, and the many more women I have yet to meet—that is who I am. That is Claes."

"Oh, really."

Loren didn't want to be impressed—and yet it was something else to observe Claes's courage in so unabashedly declaring what so many women in the world would find disgusting. One could not walk the battlefield without courage, and Loren had reasonable confidence in himself. Yet he knew that for as long as he lived, he would never reach Claes's level of self-assurance. Thus Loren was defeated; a defeat that honestly didn't bother him in the slightest. He glanced at Claes, who was busy being assaulted by his party for his brash statement.

They spent some time traveling to the sounds of these frivolous conversations. Claes suffered some truly mysterious light injuries, but apart from that, they faced no meaningful obstructions. As the sun began to tilt toward the western sky, they reached their destination.

It was about the same size as Rose's village and was structured like many other standard farming settlements. However, while there were signs that humans had lived there until recently, by the time Loren and the rest of the party arrived, it was completely abandoned.

After taking a good look around, Loren stood in the center square, glanced at the trees to the north, and said, "If something's going on, it's got to be in there."

The sky was darkening, but the forest was darker. The tree trunks were spaced wide enough to slip between, but their leaves grew in such abundance that they blocked nearly all light—and while this was certainly uncanny, if you didn't look too closely, it seemed like any other forest.

"Isn't that a little too simple? We can't deny the possibility that there could have been a monster attack." Lapis stood beside him, her hands clutching vegetables and salted meats pinched from who knew where. Loren couldn't contain the skepticism in his eyes.

"They were in this village's warehouse, but they're about to rot and wilt," she said. "Would that not be such a waste? Rather than leaving them to compost, don't you think we could put them to better use?"

"If we find any villagers, we're paying them."

There was no telling what had happened to the villagers, and Loren was quite opposed to gobbling up their valuable food stores. However, if Lapis was telling the truth, the supplies were indeed best used before they spoiled. Still, the villagers deserved to be paid in kind, and he needed to hammer this point home to Lapis, who looked like she would dine and dash without a second thought.

"Very well, if you insist," she easily conceded.

She was likely so convinced that they would never find those villagers that she wasn't worried over the thought of losing a single coin. As Loren stared at her, Lapis nonchalantly began lining up the supplies she had procured.

"They aren't exactly fresh, but it's nice to have some vegetables. We should have quite the feast tonight."

"Glad to hear it. Come to think of it, where's..." Loren cut himself off with a sigh once he saw Ange carrying a barrel and a chain of sausages from one of the houses. Then swallowed his breath once he saw Claes leading a cow from a barn. "What are you people doing?"

Loren wasn't sure what tone he'd landed on, but Claes and his party scrambled to give excuses similar to Lapis's, and Loren pressed a hand to his brow with a deep, long sigh.

He wondered if they were simply using the villagers' absence as an excuse to act like ruffians, but it was an adventurer's creed to use whatever they could—to eat whatever was available.

"You're paying the villagers, too, if we find them. You got that?"

"You're not budging on that, eh?" Claes mused.

Perhaps because it had been tethered in the barn, the cow Claes had discovered was quite emaciated. It wasn't quite starving, but it was a near enough thing that it must have gone unattended for a good while. This gave no hints as to where the villagers had gone.

"What are you planning on doing with the cow?"

"I thought we could get some milk."

"Not when it's so thin. Put it back."

"Fine. But this one's pretty lucky. The monsters and beasts didn't get to her when the villagers weren't around to keep them at bay."

Claes's casual remark sent Loren's mind wandering. The livestock at these farming villages were usually killed by monsters and beasts even when the villagers *were* around. Anything on four legs should have been easy pickings, yet the cow had been left completely unharmed long enough for it to lose all that weight.

"I'll put her back where I found her, but I can give her some food, can't I? I'd feel bad if she starved to death."

"Yeah, go ahead. Let me help you."

No matter where the villagers had up and gone to, the livestock was still alive. There was no point in letting them starve. And so Loren accompanied Claes to the barn and helped him feed the cow and its companions.

The sun set as they worked. By the time it was completely dark, they had decided to set up camp in the square. They had considered borrowing houses to spend the night in, but it was rather unsettling to sleep there when they still didn't know why or how the villagers disappeared. Everyone apart from Loren was against it.

"You guys would never make it on the battlefield. Out there, it's pretty common to sleep side by side with corpses."

"But those corpses could turn undead and attack us."

"Hey, it happens. You just have to deal with it."

As Loren said, if corpses were left carelessly unattended and new life was breathed into the dead, soldiers could find themselves on the wrong end of a zombie attack. In most cases, bodies in good condition were tied with ropes, stuffed in bags, or burned to prevent that sort of trouble.

"Asking, just for reference, but what would a body in *bad* condition look like?" Ange asked him.

"If they have no head, or their limbs were torn off. Then they either don't come back, or if they do, they can't move properly."

"Good to know," she said, looking quite disheartened. As far as Loren was concerned, this was a daily occurrence, and there was no use getting hung up on it. Or rather, he had grown so accustomed to it that he no longer felt perturbed. Of course, that unpleasant feeling didn't go away entirely, but enough experience allowed him to endure and ignore that kind of thing. "Forget about that; let's eat. We've got some nice stuff today."

"Right. We secured some supplies, and the well was in one piece, so we can use plenty of water."

During their investigations, they'd found that the well that supported the villagers' livelihoods was completely untouched.

After drawing a pail, Loren first slathered some water on his arm. He watched for a reaction for a while, then put a small amount into his mouth. He confirmed the taste, spat it out, and waited a while to make sure nothing happened. Finally, he ingested a small amount and waited to be sure. Ultimately, he decided it wouldn't be an issue.

"I'm pretty sure it's okay. We should boil it just in case."

"Understood. Shall I use *Purify*?" Lapis suggested.

"Feels like a waste, but if you're going to sleep right after, go ahead. And wait, that would make all the checks I went through pretty pointless."

"It's not that I don't trust you. But perhaps there are things I would rather not put in my mouth even if they are harmless."

This barely phased Loren. But after hearing that, Claes's party regarded the water far more cautiously.

"I can only process a set quantity of water with *Purify*. It might not cover all the water in the pot, but we can stir it and thin out the impurities as much as we can. That should lower the possibility of anyone getting sick."

The party currently had two priests. That meant double the number of blessings, but they couldn't waste too many of these limited arts just to secure drinking water.

"*Purify* is a simple blessing, so I'll use it," Lapis offered. "Let's preserve Ms. Laure's power."

That settled, she used *Purify* on the pail of water.

By Lapis's appraisal, Laure apparently exceeded her in priestly abilities. Heal blessings, and other powers that were directly correlated with the skills of their practitioners, were best preserved in case of emergency. However, Lapis freely used this one, which would turn out the same no matter what priest waved their hands to cast it.

"So is Laure the better priest here?"

"Unfortunately, yes. Solely as a priest, that is," Lapis relented, though that could have been taken any number of ways. Not that Loren could blame her. Given her true identity as a demon, Lapis's overall abilities likely outpaced Laure by leaps and bounds—but she could hardly say that in mixed company.

It seemed Laure came out ahead in terms of blessing usage count as well.

"Is it a difference in faith?"

"Yes, well, it's probably something like that," Lapis admitted, unenthusiastic. This too was understandable; Loren patted her on the head.

All the while, Lapis briskly prepared for dinner, not that she could make anything too intricate. The items procured from the village houses were chopped into bite-sized pieces and shoved into a pot also procured from one of the houses. The whole lot was boiled in water with more house-procured salt and herbs to make a modest stew. The meal was still warmer than the preserved rations they would otherwise have been chewing on, and it was a joy to savor something juicy.

For the bread, they had no choice but to use what they had on hand. The bread that remained in the village was already moldy, hardly in a state to be eaten.

"Don't you love a girl who can cook?" asked Claes, sounding incredibly optimistic and carefree in this creepy village where every human had up and disappeared.

Maybe he really is going to make it big someday, Loren thought as he coldly replied, "Make a pass at her and you'll end up in the dirt."

"I see. It's not my style to go after another man's girl."

"She's not my girl."

"Oh? Then do I have a chance...?"

The sword from Loren's back stabbed swiftly into the ground just beyond the end of Claes's toes. It was as if a black wall had manifested before his feet, and Claes's face froze in a smile.

"You say something?" Loren asked with such composure that it was hard to imagine he was the one who had just whipped out that enormous weapon.

"I'm looking forward to the meal. That's all," Claes immediately replied, unphased. Despite everything, his sheer nerve and tact were astounding.

4 Daybreak to Chaos

NIGHT GAVE WAY to morning. They had kept watch on rotation, ensuring the fire never went out. Loren and Lapis had been on the watch together when a faint light graced the eastern sky. They squinted at the blinding sunrise.

Although they understood it had been necessary to spend the night in a mysteriously abandoned village, that didn't mean they'd enjoyed it. The fact it all ended without a hitch was such a relief that they even lowered their guard a bit.

"No one came."

As far as they could tell, no one had come from the forest, and no one had left for the forest.

"What shall we do today, then?"

"For the time being, let's investigate the village again. Then we'll have to consider entering the forest. If something's up, it's got to be either here or in the trees, after all."

There wasn't anything else around. Loren had circled the village and failed to spot anything else of interest. Lapis nodded in agreement and glanced at the tent where Claes and his party were sleeping.

"Thankfully, it didn't end up as it did with Mr. Saerfé"

Loren got the feeling he remembered that name from somewhere. It took a while, but he finally recalled that this was the name of the leader of the party Lapis had been traveling with when they first met. Loren recalled exactly what the man had done in the middle of a job, and he understood Lapis's concerns. From his behavior, she had assumed that Claes was the same sort as her old leader.

"Well, he was good enough to make it to iron. He knows to pick the right time and place."

"Or perhaps he simply learned how to after enough experience."

"It doesn't matter. As long as it doesn't bother us." The nearby forest meant that the village had plenty of firewood in stock. Loren threw a log into the fire, then went to fetch more from the pile. "I guess we should get some water boiling for breakfast. Could you go wake up Claes?"

Lapis nodded. "All right."

Loren dangled a pot over the blazing fire and poured in the water. A heavy breakfast would have negative consequences throughout the day, so what he made was quite simple. He toasted thin slices of bread over the fire and melted cheese over them.

Alcohol wasn't right for the early morning. He dropped a few leaves from his supply bag into the boiling water and brewed a weak tea. That was plenty good enough for breakfast.

Just as he was finishing up, Claes and his party wormed their way out of the tent.

"You're quite the skillful man, Loren," Claes mused as he looked over the simple meal preparations. Loren didn't reply, instead urging Claes to change into his adventurer gear.

Loren never took off his equipment, even when sleeping. Everyone else in the party at the very least removed their armor and opted to sleep more comfortably. They needed to reequip themselves.

However, Claes and his party had been adventuring for long enough; the moment they were out of the tent, they began buckling on their equipment.

"We start work as soon as we're done eating. Let's investigate the village first."

"Right. Let's hope we find something relevant to this quest."

Loren held out a cup of tea, which Claes graciously accepted. He shook his head to clear away his drowsiness before taking a sip.

"You're using nice leaves. They have a fine scent."

"We had a generous financier this time, after all."

"Oh...so it's my money. Then I'll drink as much as I like."

Claes gulped down the drink with a bitter smile as Loren handed him a slice of cheese toast. He said his thanks, then realized that they were gathering the attention of the women in the party.

Claes took a bite, then tilted his head. "Are they finally realizing my charm?" he asked, flipping his hair to the side.

"Looks like someone woke up on a high horse," Loren said, regarding him tiredly. But he soon noticed the curious gaze from Lapis, and the unpleasant looks from the girls, and frowned. "What?"

"Mr. Loren, you're getting along quite well with Mr. Claes," Lapis spoke as the representative of the female voices.

Finding Ange, Leila, and Laure's eyes quite unsettling, he replied, "I'm not even doing anything. You don't have to glare at me like that."

"True, but..."

"Don't worry. I can't be friends with him unless he gets over his women problems."

"That's a relief." Lapis placed a hand to her chest and breathed out.

That seemed to settle the matter, and the rest of the girls relented with that explanation. Loren looked at Claes, who was chowing down on his bread, looking back at him with a *Do you need something?* sort of smile.

There seemed to be no use in worrying about it, so Loren carried on making preparations. He continued slicing the bread they'd received with his (carefully cleaned) knife and toasting it with cheese by the fire. He was nearly done when a voice echoed in his head.

<*Something's coming, Mister. And in large numbers.*>

He asked Scena where they were coming from, and she said it was from the west. So he set down his bread and knife and looked. The plains he could make out through the gaps between houses didn't seem to contain any of the things Scena might warn him about.

However, a Lifeless King—a being that far surpassed humanity—had gone out of her way to raise the alarm. He wasn't going to relax just because he couldn't see anything, and Loren reached for his sword that he had placed to the side.

"Mr. Loren? Is something out there?" Lapis asked as she picked up his discarded bread and took a bite.

He thought for a moment about what he ought to tell her. When he could pick up absolutely no signs himself, it was hard to imagine the party would believe him if he told them some great threat was on the way. When it came to Lapis, he only needed to mention Scena, but he couldn't tell Claes and his comrades that he had received a warning from a being such as her.

With that, he suddenly lost all potential evidence.

"I think I saw something." He was aware his words lacked all credibility but could think of nothing else.

Lapis's face turned grim; she tossed her bread aside and grabbed Ange, who was reaching out for one of the slices of toast.

"Lapis?"

"Ms. Ange, do you know how to cast *Distant View*?"

"Y-yeah, it's an elementary, fundamental spell, so of course I can cast it..."

Distant View was a simple spell that allowed one to see faraway scenery. As Ange said, it was elementary magic. Any magician should have been able to use it, and it wasn't the sort of thing Lapis should have had to specify. However, there were always magicians out there who solely specialized in combat arts and didn't learn anything else.

"Then please do so."

"You want me to look that way, right? Got it." Ange began chanting, making no effort to question Lapis's demand.

"Is something about to happen?" Claes chimed in. "I can't see a thing..."

"I don't know, but I got a bad feeling."

Loren was frustrated at the increasing vagueness of his own replies, but there was nothing he could do about it. He briefly considered exposing Scena's secret, but between some approaching unknown and a Lifeless King, it was clear which Claes would find more dangerous.

"A mercenary's instinct? Then we'd better get ready."

"You trust me?" Loren asked.

Claes shoved the last bite of his bread into his mouth and nodded. "It's an instinct tempered over countless battlefields. Why wouldn't I trust that?"

Nodding along with Claes's words, Leila and Laure immediately got to work taking down the tent. Loren felt a little bad about that, as neither had even touched breakfast yet; he wondered how he would apologize if it turned out to be nothing at all. His worries, however, were lifted by Ange and her spell.

"I see the shadows of horsemen! Their numbers... I don't know, but there are a lot!"

"Judging by the direction, they must be coming from Waargenberg. I get the feeling it shouldn't be a problem, but I'm not so keen on running into them either."

"Yeah, I don't know. But this reeks of trouble."

Loren couldn't ignore the war being fought just beyond the forest. This was probably one of the units involved in the fighting. The party had too little information to surmise what soldiers might be doing here, but they might not look too kindly on a band of adventurers cooking stolen goods from a deserted village.

Loren stomped out the fire. "Nothing good will come of being found. Ange, are they coming our way?"

They had used properly dried wood, so there hadn't been too much smoke, but even a thin trail could give away their position to the keen-eyed rider.

"They're headed straight for us."

"There's nowhere to run. We'll have to hide in one of the storehouses."

There was no telling what was in the forest, and he wanted to avoid charging in without preparation. That left the village as their only option.

"All right, we'll do what you think is best," Claes declared, voicing his immediate support.

Loren glared at his back. "Hey, you're supposed to be the leader here."

Only Loren, or rather Scena, could have known that something was approaching, so Claes couldn't have done anything there. But now that they knew soldiers were riding toward them, it was Claes's duty to take charge.

"True, but it sounds like you're more experienced."

"I'm not denying that." But still, something rubbed him wrong with the ostensible leader not weighing in at all.

Regardless of Loren's thoughts on the matter, Claes's party deftly erased any sign of their campsite without further input.

Before long, the riders Loren had sensed and Ange had seen arrived at the village. By then, the party had cleaned up their campsite and left the square behind.

At first, they considered hiding in one of the storehouses or barns, but on second thought, they realized the riders might try to scrounge up food for themselves. With that in mind, they picked one of the houses at random and hunkered down there.

That left the issue of what they would do with the donkey loaded up with all their supplies. Deciding he would apologize and explain the situation if the villagers returned, Loren led the donkey into the house with them.

"They have nice equipment."

Loren raised the shutters just high enough that it wouldn't be suspicious and peered through the gap. Given their approach and appearance, he could still assume they were Waargenberg soldiers, but there was always a small chance that they were well-kitted bandits.

However, in that case, it would mean they were a bandit brigade capable of providing horses for several dozen men, and he didn't even want to consider bandits groups out there with such power.

"They're part of Waargenberg's standing army. No doubt about that," Leila confirmed. If a knight of Waargenberg said so, that left little room for doubt.

"What are Waargenberg soldiers doing here?" Ange asked.

"That I don't know. It must have to do with the war," Leila answered as the horsemen outside entered the village and several of their riders split off. They were presumably surveying the area and confirming the situation. That alone wasn't enough to give away their intentions.

"It would be easy to figure out if we could nab one of them."

Hearing the truth from the horse's mouth would be the quickest solution. But if they did that, they would be branded as criminals. These soldiers were surely operating under orders from the kingdom.

"Should we sneakily take one?" Lapis proposed.

Loren shook his head. "And who's gonna do that? It would either be me or Claes, and then we'd have the whole kingdom on our tails."

"Can't we do anything with your connections, Ms. Leila?"

Leila was still reeling from the proposition of kidnapping. As the question was posed to her, she tightened her expression and thought, but ultimately shook her head with a groan. "That would be difficult. I don't know if they'd listen or not. If they're on a secret mission, we could be arrested on the spot."

"That doesn't sound so bad to me," Loren muttered.

He wasn't keen on this job to begin with. Being apprehended by an overwhelming force of kingdom soldiers was a perfectly justifiable reason to give up. Even so, he didn't want to be tied up if he could avoid it. He wouldn't mind so much if it was just him, but he didn't want Lapis or anyone else to go through that experience.

"It would be easier if I saw a familiar face..." Leila whispered. "No, wait. That's probably..." She drew her face closer to the window and focused her eyes, staring at the riders a while longer to ensure she was remembering correctly. "I spotted someone who might hear us out. I'll head out first. If it works, I'll come get you. Otherwise, I'll shout, and you'll have to run. Nothing much will happen to me should I be detained."

She left before anyone could question her. They could only see her off in silence rather than risk giving themselves away. Loren and Lapis took up the donkey's leads, prepared to run at any time as they turned their ears to the noises outside.

Leila was surrounded as soon as she exposed herself. But perhaps she introduced herself as a knight of Waargenberg, as she was not restrained, but instead led to the square where the horsemen gathered.

"Do you think Leila will be all right?" Ange anxiously asked.

Claes put a hand to her shoulder and pulled her closer to reassure her. Laure looked at them enviously, so Claes reached a hand around her hips and reeled her in as well.

"What are you people doing..."

Loren wondered if they really understood the situation, only to notice Lapis looking up at him as if she expected something.

He scratched his head. "No, I'm not doing that."

"In that regard, you're losing to Mr. Claes, Mr. Loren."

"It's not about winning or losing. I'm not trying to win—and wait, consider where we are. We need to run as soon as we hear Leila's warning."

Claes bitterly released Ange and Laure, and they both immediately inched away from him with flushed cheeks. Though Lapis still looked dissatisfied, she left it at that, holding her breath as she quietly observed the events transpiring.

Eventually, they heard Leila's voice from outside.

"We talked it over! You can come out now!"

Claes breathed a sigh of relief. However, Lapis remained tense, and Loren kept a vigilant hand on his sword.

"Loren? What's wrong?" asked Claes. "Leila says it's all right..."

"Don't take everything at face value. I'll go first."

It was his and Lapis's creed to never let their guard down until they knew for sure that everything was all right. However, he didn't expect Claes to understand, so Loren decided to head out first. Should something happen, he could buy enough time for the others to get away.

Although he didn't seem to understand what Loren was worried about, Claes blankly nodded.

Loren pushed open the door and found several soldiers waiting for him. They seemed surprised to see Loren with his hand on his sword, but Leila raced over.

"As I thought, you took point. It's all right, it really is," she told him.

"You're not going to tell me to drop my weapon, are you?"

"No, you're fine. But don't go on a rampage. There's no telling how much havoc you'd wreak if you ran amok. I, Dame Leila, shall guarantee your safety."

If she was leaning on the knight thing, it was probably all right. He finally took his hand off his sword. A wave of relief washed over the gathered soldiers as he turned around and locked eyes with Lapis through the gap in the door. He beckoned for her to emerge.

Once they all piled out, one of the soldiers asked them, "Could you come with me? I will take you to our leader." He started off and urged them to follow.

They were led into the midst of the riders on standby in the square and gathered around one man in particular.

"I apologize for speaking down to you from horseback. My name is Karl Bernadotte. I am taking charge here as a knight who has pledged loyalty to the Kingdom of Waargenberg."

He was a middle-aged man in armor even more splendid than that of his peers. He sported a fine beard and his eyes, which peered down at them from atop his horse, were somewhat wary, but not unpleasant.

Loren returned his greeting. He knew that it was only good manners to exchange a name for a name. "Loren. Adventurer. Circumstances brought us here."

In the kingdom, knights were an extension of the nobility. Loren didn't think the man would even stop to acknowledge an adventurer, but there didn't seem to be any dismissal in Karl's eyes.

"It is a pleasure. I heard a bit about those circumstances from Dame Leila—you are investigating the abnormalities of this village at the behest of the nearby settlement. Is that correct?"

"That's mostly right."

It didn't feel quite right to say he was here at Rose's behest. To be more precise, his temporary party leader had fallen for her womanly wiles. Not that he had any intentions of explaining that to a sworn paragon of chivalry.

It was pointless to do so, and moreover shameful to expose the sort of person his party leader was, even if he only answered to Claes for now. On top of that, it should have been Claes talking to the knight, but Loren didn't want Claes getting taken advantage of again. He was stuck taking the initiative.

"That man there is...Sir Claes. I've heard the rumors—that he was an excellent adventurer." Karl glanced behind Loren, lowering his head a bit to Claes, who reciprocated the respectful nod.

"What brings you here, Knight of Waargenberg?" Claes asked.

"That is a confidential military matter, so I cannot say. But we intend to enter the forest and head north."

Wouldn't that be confidential too? thought Loren. Since the war was being fought beyond the trees, Karl's men were surely planning on navigating the forest to flank the enemy. He couldn't see any other option.

It wasn't wise to traverse a forest on horseback, but the trees weren't too densely packed. As long as they didn't try for a full gallop, it seemed safe enough.

"But there was something bothering me, you see, and those nagging doubts have only grown stronger since coming here."

"Are you able to tell us what those doubts are?" Lapis asked before Loren could open his mouth.

Karl's face turned wary for a moment, but it softened once she saw that the question came from a pretty girl in priest robes.

Those vestments are really convenient at times like these, thought Loren.

"Do you know that a war is being fought nearby?"

"Yes, we've heard."

"Truth be told, there are soldiers deserting from both sides, one after another."

That's nothing rare, Loren thought. Very few people in the world fought in wars because they wanted to. Most were forcibly conscripted, and once they realized they could die at any second, they understandably wanted to get the hell out.

It was curious how Karl mentioned it was happening to both sides, mind. However, whether you were on the winning side or the losing one, that didn't change much with regard to your statistical likelihood of a painful death. Even victorious soldiers didn't necessarily want to stick around.

"Well, it seems that those deserters all ran into this forest." Karl glared sharply at the trees. "So I was sure they had fled to the village beyond it, but if the village is empty, then I have to wonder where they've gone."

"Is it possible they stopped somewhere inside?"

"I don't know. We have not the time nor the men to spare for the investigation." And there, Karl turned to Loren with a proposition. "It's up to you, but would you like to accompany us? With the village abandoned, I presume you will investigate the forest next."

"I'm not gonna join your war."

"I'm not asking you to. However, I'm sure you'll learn something if you venture into the forest with us, and don't you think we'll have more safety in numbers? We certainly wouldn't mind the extra pairs of capable hands."

While knights and soldiers focused primarily on combat, adventurers were better at scouting and detecting danger. In exchange for those abilities, Karl would allow them to borrow the strength of his soldiers while in the forest.

The terms weren't terrible, but there was probably a catch. Loren stared back at Karl, who patiently awaited his answer.

In the end, Loren decided to take Karl up on his offer. He'd already told the man that he wasn't about to enlist, and if Karl tried to change his mind, Loren would just feign ignorance until this damn quest was over, no matter what anyone said. Whatever was happening in the forest, it would be better to tackle it with more people.

Ideally, he would have made his decision after consulting with Claes. However, Claes simply assented the moment Loren brought it up, and his party members didn't complain. Thus, it was decided.

"Will we be on foot?"

"I'm sorry, but we don't have any spare horses. We will be proceeding slowly, so it shouldn't be an issue."

Even if he was lent a horse, Loren had hardly any riding experience. Mercenaries didn't tend to—horses were quite expensive to upkeep. Warhorses even more so, and they were incredibly hard to come across outside of a national army.

It was the same with Claes, and in fact only Leila—and for some reason Lapis—had ever ridden a warhorse before.

"When did you ever ride one?" Loren asked.

"Yes, well, that's a lady's secret. Can't we keep it at that?" Lapis laughed it off, ambiguous as ever. They weren't getting horses in any case, so it didn't really matter, and Loren decided not to pester her.

Karl left a few of his horsemen in the village. He thought perhaps the villagers might return, and he sent messengers to inform the main army of the strange happenings.

If that gets the country moving, maybe the situation will resolve itself, thought Loren. But that didn't mean they could turn back.

"Then let's go."

On Karl's order, the horsemen began their slow trot through the forest. The adventurers walked at the front near Karl.

It was dark among the trees, but not so dense that it would impede a horse. The paths were more than wide enough for humans, and Karl ordered the riders to proceed two abreast.

"How wide is the forest?"

"Just about a stound or so, traversable on foot within a day."

Soldiers were generally knowledgeable as to the lay of the land. Maps were available to the public, but they were hardly precise things, and the nation often kept exact details and distances a secret.

"Still, there's something strange about it," Karl muttered, looking around. "Have you noticed? A proper forest should be teeming with birds, bugs, and beasts, but I hear no traces of life. It's too quiet."

Loren didn't need to have this pointed out to him. A forest was an ecosystem, home to all sorts of lifeforms. It was disquieting not to sense, hear, or see them. There weren't even any birds when he looked to the sky, and not a single animal scampered across their path.

"The deserters and the missing villagers should be in here somewhere."

"But it's uncanny that there's absolutely no trace of them," Lapis said, thinking aloud.

The soldiers must have been thinking the same. A few of the horsemen looked around anxiously.

"I would investigate, given the time," said Karl. "But I have my orders."

"It's never a good sign when the soldiers are wound up," muttered Loren.

"It will all be over once we make it out."

However, they soon reached a point where they had to halt.

About half a stound into the forest, a horseman sent to scout ahead returned. "Reporting in! We spotted a human farther down the road!"

Karl immediately ordered his men to halt, forming a small party to confirm this and racing at its lead. Loren and the rest of his party joined them.

Soon, they met with a perplexed soldier pointing at a figure standing stock-still. Once Karl approached the soldier, he reported, "A human, Captain."

"A villager?"

The figure—seemingly a woman—did not seem to react to the horsemen. Her clothes were the sort any villager might wear, and she didn't seem to be armed.

As she was still a good distance away, and the forest was dim, it was impossible to see what sort of face she was making. But her body didn't sway; she was just planted to the spot. Ominous.

"*Is* she human?" Loren muttered at the sight.

In his head, Scena replied, <*She's at least not undead, Mister.*>

Do you sense anything else around?

<*I...can't really tell. Maybe and maybe not...*>

This only made Loren even warier. It was certainly not normal when even a Lifeless King was stuck on maybe.

<*It's like someone is obstructing my senses. Be careful.*>

He needed no further prompting. At the sight of Loren reaching for his blade, his agitation spread to Lapis and Claes's party as well. Even Karl barked out new orders.

"Be on your toes! There's no telling what will happen!"

The change came in that very instant. The first sign was a sweet scent tickling Loren's nostrils, as though there was honey mixed in with the very air he breathed. Loren immediately covered his mouth, but he couldn't stop himself from inhaling.

"Wh-what is this?"

Karl's cry of dismay sounded strangely distant as Loren smacked his own chest.

Each time he inhaled this sickly sweetness, a haze crept further over his mind. Before he knew it, Loren had fallen to his knees.

The horsemen were similarly affected, and some began toppling from their hoses in a daze.

"Are you all right, Mr. Loren?"

He couldn't stop himself from breathing, but each inhale made him hazier and hazier. He could hear an alarm in his head telling him to get away that instant, but his limbs wouldn't listen to him.

Yet despite all his struggles, there stood Lapis by his side, looking surprisingly normal. She stuck a hand under his arm and lifted him to his feet.

"It's getting quite strange around here."

She was talking right beside him, yet it sounded like she was somewhere far away. It was as if he were in a deep, drunken stupor, and though he desperately shook his head to regain clarity, each new lungful of air put him back where he started. It was difficult to even stand on his own.

"Lapis...you're fine?"

"Yes, pretty much. As expected of me. You can praise me if you like," she said with a smile.

She wrapped an arm around his waist, and he borrowed her shoulder to steady his staggering feet. As his mind started to drift, he could barely piece his words together.

"The...others?"

"The ladies were no good. They're all down for the count. Mr. Claes is...that's incredible. He looks fine."

"The horsemen..."

"Absolutely useless. Most fell off their horses, and they're all lying about."

"I...see..."

Loren couldn't collect his thoughts; his breathing was becoming erratic. Realizing he was overly conscious of Lapis's body pressed against his, for a moment, Loren wondered what he was thinking. He used his free hand to deliver a smack to his own cheek.

With that movement, he managed to cut the inside of his mouth against his teeth, and the pain and the blood snapped him back to reality for a fleeting moment. But he was quickly cast into the fog again.

"What is this...?"

"Who knows? I'd...reckon we're in quite the pickle here. Wouldn't you agree?" Lapis finally sounded worried, further proof that they were in quite the predicament.

But any solution Loren could dredge up was carried off by the sweet scent flooding into his mouth and nose. "Poison..."

"I don't think it is. But hey, it immediately breached all the protections I put on you, so whoever's doing it's got to be quite the fiend," Lapis answered as she took a sweeping look around. She clicked her tongue. "Even worse, we're surrounded."

Human figures began appearing from the shadows of the trees—so many that Loren had no idea where they had all been hiding. Some looked like villagers, others like soldiers, and they varied in form and gender. Slowly, they trudged forward and grabbed the fallen men, dragging them off farther into the forest.

Surprised that the horses weren't spooked into a panic, Lapis waved a distracted hand at one of the figures. Just like that, the head of the person about to grab her was torn off like a doll's and sent flying beyond the trees. Blood burst from the body that remained behind.

The smell of blood awakened Loren ever so slightly. "Run..."

"That's a hard one. Hey, Claes!" Lapis called, and Claes, who was trying to rouse his party members, turned to her. Either from Lapis's new tone, or the situation, or everything combined, his face was stained with shock. "Can you run?" she asked him.

"I-I don't know. But I can't leave my party."

"I should think not. Why don't you try one of the horses?"

"What about the soldiers?"

"Leave them. It would be impossible to save them all."

Thus ordered to hurry, Claes quickly slung Ange, Laure, and Leila over the back of one of the stationary horses.

Another figure approached Lapis, and this one she toppled with a kick. The next, she grabbed by the lapels and slammed into the trunk of a tree. Easily hoisting Loren onto a horse, she leaped into the saddle behind him.

"It would be nice if this was something we could outrun, but that doesn't seem to be the case, does it?"

"Which way do we go?!" Claes cried. With three piled on a horse's back, there was no place for a rider. Claes had little choice but to grab the reins and pull it along.

Lapis shrugged. "Yes, that is the issue. We need to get away, for one. Let's go."

"Got it. I'll follow your lead!"

Lapis worried what she would do if the horse wouldn't run for her. But after a light kick to its belly, the beast obediently broke into gallop. Any other man left to follow her would have been abandoned in the dust, but Claes used *Boost* on himself to augment his legs.

THE Strange Adventure OF A Broke MERCENARY

5 From Bedlam to Battle

THE HORSE RAN FOR HER, but not at full speed. Its heart didn't seem to be in it, but Lapis was grateful that it moved at all.

Loren, slung over its back, drifted halfway between dreams and reality. At times, he would grit his teeth and strike himself to remain lucid, but with little success.

"Don't push it. Go to sleep."

"Lapis..."

When she glanced over her shoulder, she was jolted to her core. Loren gazed at her with blatant, evident desire. She couldn't stop her face from turning red, but she needed to be sure.

"Loren, I don't want to believe it, but..." she timidly asked.

"Shut up...it's nothing..." Loren said, uncharacteristically bashful, then pressed his face into the horse's flank. There was a cracking sound as he repeatedly thrust a fist into his skull.

She knew she had to stop him, but that look of his—it gave her an inkling as to what was going on. She couldn't help even if she wanted to. Ultimately, it was a shriek from Claes that caused her to stop.

"Hold on! Now's not the—whoa?!"

Lapis turned her whole horse around to see Claes's party members reaching out from atop the horse to grab him. He tried desperately to shake them off. Ange's eyes were drowsy, intoxicated, and she slipped off of the horse to cling to Claes instead. Before he knew it, Leila had tumbled off the other side and wrapped her arms around his waist, while Laure was on the ground clinging to his feet. In this momentary lapse, his horse took off like a shot.

Considering the situation, Lapis might have yelled at them, but she couldn't after seeing the state Loren was in. Something was clearly making the impossible possible.

"Now what to do about this," she mused.

Strangely, the thought of saving Claes did not occur to her. Her concern was Loren.

She could make a guess as to his problem. If she let this continue, Loren would presumably be able to cling to reality with his abnormal levels of mental fortitude, but that risked leaving him with brain damage. *Why don't I just let it happen?* Lapis thought for a moment. But she quickly shook off the idea.

She wouldn't turn him down if he came to her, but if it happened in a way Loren didn't desire, well, that would cause no end of troubles in their relationship. More importantly, she wasn't sure how they'd manage on top of a horse in the middle of a forest.

"I'm not asking for my first time to be on a canopied bed, but..." she quipped as she smacked Loren on the back. "Scena, can you hear me? If you can, then take control of him for a bit. I'm sure you should be able to do that. If anything happens to him, I'll apologize for you."

Loren's body twitched. After a moment, he sat up and turned with no expression on his face. It was a tad unpleasant to meet his hollow-eyed stare, but Lapis locked eyes with him and asked, "Did it work?"

"Yes, ma'am..." He spoke in Loren's voice, but not with Loren's words. His tone was level, yet it sent a chill down Lapis's spine.

"So it's you, Scena?"

"Mister willingly gave over control," Loren's mouth replied, though he was clearly someone else.

Of course, it went without saying that this someone else was the Lifeless King Scena, who usually laid low within Loren. Under normal circumstances, even a Lifeless King wouldn't be able to snatch the reins of someone else's body, not without a struggle. Loren, cognizant of his own strange behavior, had given his body up willingly and enabled a simple switch.

"Any difficulties moving your limbs?"

Scena had originally been human, but she'd been dropped into a very different physique. Though the general principle behind moving would remain, the difference in perspective offered by Loren's hulking build meant she might need some time to acclimate.

"I don't feel anything off. But I don't think I can fight, ma'am," Scena answered, looking over herself curiously and twisting her arms and neck.

She might still possess Loren's innate physical strength, but hefting his greatsword didn't mean she had the skills necessary to wield the thing. She could only hope to flail it around at random, which, while intimidating, was hardly the same thing as fighting at Loren's level.

"And I wouldn't recommend we stay like this for long." Scena went on to explain that exerting control over a body other than one's own would have terrible effects on its owner. Perhaps there would be consequences for Loren's astral body as well, seeing as it had been temporarily severed from his physical form. If possible, this swap had to be kept short.

"Then, worst-case scenario, we forget about everything and run," said Lapis. "Otherwise, you return control to Loren, and I'll take him on."

"So you'll stand and fight." Scena said with a face of admiration. "That's so mature of you!"

The way she spoke through Loren created such a gap between behavior and appearance that Lapis could feel her head spinning. "D-do you feel anything else?" she asked.

"Yes, well. Umm...I feel a little uncomfortable. How should I put it..."

Scena fidgeted while lowering her gaze southward. That was enough for Lapis to infer what she meant, and she looked to the sky with a deep sigh. The difference in build between the two was certainly a problem, but more so was the fact that Loren was a man, and Scena was not.

In short, he was equipped in ways she wasn't, and she found

the sensation of these new organs to be rather confusing and unpleasant.

"I've determined we are in quite the predicament."

"M-ma'am...?"

"I must collect adequate data on the matter..."

"Anything but that, ma'am. You're going to kill him spiritually." Scena flapped her hands. It would have been cute if it was a little girl doing it, but Loren's trained arms were lethal weapons. As she thrashed around on horseback, Lapis had to soothe the beast's troubled grunts.

"Sorry, sorry. It was just a bit of a joke," Lapis apologized.

"Seriously, give me a break. He can hear our conversation, you know."

Lapis's face twitched at that. Through Loren's senses, Scena could always see and hear what was going on in the world. Apparently, the situation had been reversed, and she was now sending information to him.

"Since I became undead, I've been fine with floating about in a pitch-black abyss. But Mister is human, so he'll suffer psychologically if I deprive him of his senses for too long."

"I believe I've heard of a torture like that."

"That's why I'm making sure to share my eyes and ears. Please consider that before you say anything."

"I'll take that to heart."

Lapis shuddered a bit; there was no telling what retribution she would face when all was said and done. Then she glanced at Claes, who was still struggling on the ground. The man was

putting up a desperate resistance, and in terms of strength he had the advantage. But it was three against one, and it was hard to say he had the upper hand.

"That's a surprise. I thought you would go with the flow and get it on with them," she said.

"Even I know how to choose the right time and place!"

Though Claes did his best to tear them away, he couldn't bear to treat his own comrades too roughly. What's more, they showed absolutely no consideration for the circumstances, audaciously sticking their hands into the gaps under his armor and running their tongues down his neck and arms.

"And I wouldn't be happy doing it with them when it's like they've been drugged!"

"I don't really know how to react to that."

"I'm begging you! Do something!"

Seeing Claes begging for help as he was overwhelmed by women was probably a rare sight, one Lapis would never see again if she let this chance slip by. However, now wasn't the time to be entertained.

"I'll be a bit rough. Don't think ill of me." She waved her hand before he could reply. Then Claes and the three girls coiled around him were sent flying straight into the grove.

Claes remained conscious, and the girls had cushioned the blow, so he was up in no time. The other three weren't so lucky; they writhed in pain and had taken too much damage to stand.

"What was that...? Rather, wasn't that a bit too violent?"

"I sent the lot of you flying with a *Force* blessing. And don't say I didn't warn you. I didn't have time to restrain them."

Force was one of the few blessings that had nothing to do with healing, support, or defense. It delivered as much damage as an unseen fist would, but it definitely didn't have enough firepower to send four people flying.

"It's a bit late, but can I ask...who you are, exactly?" Claes muttered.

"I'm just a priest of the god of knowledge. How 'bout you leave it at that?"

Lapis's tone made Claes quickly realize that his question was entering forbidden territory. He clenched his teeth against the pain Lapis had inflicted and nodded.

"Anyways, we need to find who's behind all this and put an end to it once and for all."

Lapis pressed on farther into the forest with Loren's body following behind. She could have brought Claes as a reserve force—after all, he could move even under these circumstances—but that left the issue of his party members, who were under the spell. He refused to leave them lying on the ground, but moving with three unconscious and volatile people would destroy their mobility. Taking him along was therefore more trouble than it was worth.

With little choice in the matter, Lapis ordered Claes to watch over his girls and went on with Loren (or rather, Scena). For what it was worth, Scena at least had Loren's strength and stamina and could keep up with Lapis's pace.

"Ma'am, umm, you know—"

"How about you stop calling me ma'am?" Lapis cut her off, stopped, and looked back, her face was caught between anger and confusion.

"Is ma'am no good?"

"Yes, well, it would probably be fine if you were the one saying it, but you look like Mr. Loren right now. It feels uncomfortable to be called that by a trained swordsman who's taller than me."

Lapis's tone was back to usual, and Scena was too flustered to realize it.

"But ma'am, I can't talk like Mister does."

"I'm not telling you to imitate him, but...can't we do something about this?"

It chipped away at Lapis's will, dampened her motivation, and really, Scena's manner of talking was more troublesome to Lapis than whatever was happening in the forest. It was so serious, in fact, that she wouldn't have the energy to face the culprit if it wasn't dealt with first.

"I'll, umm...do my best?"

"I'm counting on you. It ties directly into my willpower."

"So, umm, err...Ms. Lapis? I think there's something we have to do before we deal with the source."

Scena struggled to settle on a tone Lapis might approve of, but this would have to be good enough. Lapis nodded and urged her on. Usually, she wouldn't welcome someone with Loren's face adding a "Miss" to her name, but she didn't need Scena deciding they were best buddies either.

"Unless we do something about the missing villagers and soldiers, we'll be greatly outnumbered when we confront whoever is behind it."

"I'm not so sure about that," Lapis countered.

She said this so quick, and so sure of herself, that Scena had to tilt her head.

"Yes, about what's going on here," Lapis went on. "It doesn't look like anyone's being *controlled* by anyone, so to speak. Regardless of who's behind it, I don't think they can move these people around like tokens on a gameboard."

"This is mental manipulation, right? Then doesn't that mean someone is controlling them?"

Scena had come to her own conclusions. This abnormality had been bad enough to incapacitate her host, and she needed to get him back to normal if she wanted to ensure her safety. As far as she could tell, whatever had assailed the armies and villages had done something to mess with their minds. She assumed the ringleader was taking control over whoever fell to the effect of what they'd done, but Lapis didn't quite see it that way.

"I don't think it's that sort of corruption," said Lapis. She started walking again and spoke in a guiding tone. "If they were being controlled, we would see some order, some goal being pursued by the enthralled. Otherwise, that control would serve no purpose whatsoever."

Put simply, Lapis didn't think it was possible to order people to act with such disorder. If the victims really were able to be bossed around, there would be some sense underlying their actions. Before swapping with Scena, Loren had looked as though he was desperately holding back something uncontrollable yet innate to him, and it was hard to imagine he could have been manipulated while in that state.

"Then you mean to say some factor is making everyone...go crazy, then?"

"Is there any relevant information left inside Mr. Loren?" Lapis asked, her hope faint.

Scena shook her head. "I take care not to share Mister's senses very often. I felt he was terribly anxious before I swapped, but I don't know exactly what state of mind he was in."

"I see, I had a bit of hope... But I expected to be disappointed."

"So you guessed as much."

Lapis looked a little proud of herself as she stuck out her chest. Perhaps Loren would have had something to say about that gesture, but he was unfortunately absent. Scena patiently waited for what Lapis had to say next, and that triumphant face soon gave way to a resigned sigh.

"This is hard..."

"Huh? Eh? Did I do something wrong?"

"Mr. Loren would have told me that was nothing to be proud about."

"I'm sorry, Ms. Lapis... I'll do my best." Scena clenched her fist and hyped herself up. It was a gesture that simply looked uncanny, coming from Loren.

"Forget about it. Anyways, I was hoping to have something to back up my hypothesis. From what I saw in Ms. Ange and her merry mistresses, it seems something is making their sexual drive run rampant."

"Sexual what?"

"The desire of a man to do his best when he pushes down a pretty woman at night, or the desire of a woman to make a mess while grappling with a pretty gentleman."

Scena didn't seem to understand much of that. Lapis thought she had offered quite a simple explanation, but Scena's next question caused her to freeze in place.

"Ms.…Lapis. Do you want to do something like that?"

"What I want at the moment is the least of our worries."

The question was so sincere and pure that Lapis quickly changed the topic. She was irritated that she couldn't think up anything clever on the spot, and knowing that she had been thrown off by a question from a girl who was several years younger than her had her face heating up.

"A-anyways, I'm getting the feeling that this is more carnal lust than it is sexual drive. Since we've had a run-in with sloth and gluttony already, I do have a vague idea of what we're dealing with…"

"Are you all right, Ms. Lapis? Your face is bright red."

"Moving on! I don't think the villagers or soldiers will be ordered to attack us, so we can put off dealing with them," she declared. Her glare ensured Scena didn't dig any further. "And with that said, finding this ringleader takes top priority."

"I see… But Ms. Lapis, and I find this hard to say…"

"What is it? Hard to say or not, it could be important. Please don't hesitate." As a matter of fact, Lapis couldn't stand to lose any information, especially not for such paltry reasons.

Scena pointed at the trees. "We're surrounded by quite a few of the not-ringleaders already."

"Huh? Don't tell me..." Lapis's gaze darted around.

She had been so sure no one was watching or listening. Only now did she realize that there were several figures standing between the trees, and she could tell they were all completely unhinged.

"How could I have..."

"Don't worry Ma...Ms. Lapis! Do your best! Everyone makes mistakes."

"I can feel my strength draining away when you speak like that with that face...enough. I should relieve some stress on them," Lapis said, sounding halfway to desperate as she clenched her right fist.

Since the plan was to stand and fight rather than turn tail and run, Scena reached for the sword on her back and hoisted it from its sheath. Regardless of who was in control, Loren's well-trained arm allowed her to wield it. Scena was severely lacking on a technical level, but muscle memory would at least let her walk at their enemy swinging.

"Until Mister comes back, I won't let you lay a single finger on Ms. Lapis!"

The wind howled as Scena performed a test swing through the air. Scena readied herself, taking a stance, only to lose her breath as she saw the figure that emerged from behind the trees. The same could have been said for Lapis, who gulped.

There were twenty-odd people around them, but the problem lay in their attire.

"Wh-why..." Lapis could not finish her own question, and understandably so.

The ones who appeared were all men, and from their clothes, they were a mix of villagers and soldiers. While their upper bodies looked somewhat normal, none wore even a shred of clothing below the waist—meaning their dangling bits were out for the world to see.

Lapis was too flabbergasted to speak, and Scena had to switch to a one-handed grip as she used her other hand to hide her eyes.

"What's going on, Ms. Lapis?!"

"Don't ask me...maybe they're so influenced by lust they're always ready to go? Or maybe they just finished and didn't bother to put anything back on?"

"Wh-wh-wh-what do we do?! I can't fight while looking at that!"

Scena was young, and originally a well-to-do lass. It was too much to ask her to fight men with their bait and tackle swinging in the breeze. Meanwhile, Lapis wasn't confident she could maintain her cool if Loren lost his mind and joined the ranks of brazen nudists.

"Let's go! We need to regroup somewhere."

"Understood. One of those strategic retreats, right?"

They were more running away than they were retreating, but once Lapis had decided upon something, she was quick to act. She immediately used her *Force* to open a hole in the surrounding forces, took Scena by the hand, and bolted.

Lapis raced through the dim forest. Her face was marked by fear. When she looked back, she could see Loren running with his sword propped against his shoulder, yet the fear had reached his face as well.

Loren rarely showed such emotion. Lapis had to marvel a little. *Is this what he looks like when he's afraid?* Not that it would prove much use as a reference. She shrugged it off and returned her attention to the path.

After all, it was Scena piloting Loren's body, and his expressions resembled hers more than his own. Though they used the same face, Loren would surely express his fear differently.

"Did they chase us?"

"We are *being chased* in the present tense!"

Monsters on their tail would have been one thing. Lapis had resolved to slaughter beasts from the moment she decided to be an adventurer. If it was an army, or even another adventurer chasing her, a battle would have been both simple and inevitable. She was a demon, after all.

However, despite everything, Lapis had never expected to be chased around a forest by countless insane disrobed men. It was too strange a challenge to face head-on.

"Why do I have to go through this?!" she protested.

"Maybe your karma caught up to you?"

"Are you saying I'm a bad person?! Are you picking a fight?!"

You'll just run out of breath faster if you shout while running, thought Scena. But Lapis, blessed with the high physical capability of a demon, was hardly worried about maintaining both a brisk run and her string of complaints.

A fresh pair of hands burst from the sides of the trees blocking their path, and Lapis planted a fist into the face of the man they belonged to, sending a spray of red across the branches.

"It's peculiar how we can't shake them off. How are they outmaneuvering us?!"

"Are we running through proper space?" pondered Scena.

As the man flew backward and fell, Lapis made sure he stayed down with a high kick. No matter how physically capable she was, it was a bit much to deliver a high kick to the back of someone's head while running.

However, if she wanted to kick more easily, she had to go for a front kick, which would most naturally be aimed at her foe's lower body. Given their foes' state of deshabille, that meant her kicks might land at that most indescribable of vital points. Lapis was just fine giving a guy what-for over his clothing, but she had absolutely no desire to risk sullying her foot.

All that aside, Lapis lingered on Scena's words and asked, "What do you mean?"

"Since Mister is like this, I believe we are already under the influence of whoever is causing this strange phenomenon. In that case, we might be trapped in some sort of domain made to prevent us from escaping."

"In short?"

"Even if we are running as hard as we can, we might just be running in circles."

"If that's the case, I'd have expected to catch up to our pursuers, then."

"When they're out of sight, they might be slipping behind the trees to catch us when we pass by. It is a vicious cycle."

Lapis hadn't stopped to memorize the face of everyone chasing them. Perhaps it really was a cycle of ambushes and chases, with just a small portion constantly on their tail. Scena's proposition was certainly plausible, but that gave way to a new problem, and one that irritated Lapis to no end.

Lapis scratched her head. "Doesn't that mean it's pointless no matter how much we run?"

"We will eventually run out of strength, and they will catch us."

When Lapis and Scena were running with all their might, their pursuers simply ran a bit and hid. It was clear who would fall first. Lapis was a demon, but it was impossible for her to outlast mindless pursuers who could stop for a breather.

"Then we need to intercept them somewhere."

"Either that or escape the domain we're trapped in."

Neither option sounded simple. Even so, they didn't have much of a choice, and Lapis steeled herself.

"For now, let's deal with these pursuers."

"I'm not confident, but I'll...huh?" Scena's voice cut off.

Lapis looked back, wondering if something had happened to her, only to see her holding her head, her childish expression changing to one far grimmer and more menacing.

"You should...leave that stuff to me!"

Her voice had changed once more, to a tone far more familiar.

"Mr. Loren?!" Lapis cried.

With the change of expression, Loren turned to face the men chasing them. Though Lapis tried to warn him, he raised his sword faster than she could call out. With a rending roar, he swung.

The blade cut deep into the trunk of the nearest tree, but that hardly even slowed it. It bit into the body of one of the men and scattered blood, flesh, and all other sorts of things as the man's upper half split into the air.

Though they saw the man's clothed half clearly parted from his naked lower body, his fellows showed no sign of fear. They jumped at Loren with all their momentum, grappling an armed foe with their bare hands. This was the definition of reckless.

"Don't touch me!"

A swing from bottom to top tore one man from crotch to crown. On the return swing, Loren reversed the move to split another from skull to sphincter. The halved bodies slowly collapsed to both sides, and as he was bathed in the blood splatter, Loren lurched to one side.

Perhaps seeing his crumbling stance as an opportunity, more men came at him with even more force, but even with his awkward positioning, and only his right hand on his sword, every foe

in the way of his massive blade found themselves easy targets to be ripped into all manner of exciting pieces.

Loren fell to his knees as more blood filled the air. Lapis raced over to him, only for Loren to hold up a hand to stop her.

"Mr. Loren! You're still affected... You have to switch out!"

His spirit was still under the influence of whatever power covered the forest. Lapis could tell in an instant that he had used the mental strain of battle to distract himself from it. But if he stayed like this for too long, its effects would eventually overpower him.

Ignoring Lapis's warning, Loren refused to hand over control to Scena. "I can't send an amateur off to kill people. Her magic has kept her distant, but she'd remember this blood on her hands."

Scena had surpassed mere humanity, but she was still a young girl. Even if there was no other option, to act here, that young girl would need to experience the sensation of a blade cleaving through flesh. She would need to experience the smell of the blood and excrement that spilled out with death. And she would know, forever, the feeling of taking a life with her own two hands.

"Just leave it to me. I'll stay sane until we're done here."

"What about after that...?"

"If I go crazy, then run. If that doesn't work..." Loren glanced at Lapis, but immediately returned his gaze to his enemies. "Get rid of me. I won't resent you for it."

"There's..." *There's no way I could do that,* Lapis was about to say. But Loren rushed out before she could.

He swung his sword down from his shoulder in a high arc, pulverizing the head of the man he struck. Loren clicked his tongue at the result—a moment ago, he had properly bisected two of them, but this time his target was messily crushed.

He wasn't in peak form; his mind and body weren't cooperating. He was swinging without finesse, simply smashing with his brute strength and the weight of his sword. But he couldn't stop now. As the man with the smashed-in head teetered but remained upright, Loren kicked the body aside and searched out his next mark.

His vision swayed, and he grit his teeth against it. Even as he fought, the sweet scent invaded his chest, mixed with the thick stench of blood in the air.

<*Don't force yourself, Mister! Switch out with me!*> Scena called to him, but Loren couldn't accept that. Instead, he made a plea. He asked her to use her energy drain ability to supply him with power.

Scena didn't ask why. She just got to work sucking mana and life force from their pursuers—from the forest itself, even—and sending it straight to Loren. He felt the external power flooding into him and used it to drag out part of himself that usually stayed buried until the very last.

"I'll make it so this doesn't shake me any more... Make sure my head's full of nothing but battle."

As if he were casting a spell on himself, Loren thought of nothing but his foes and the sword in his hand. Those were the only things he needed, and every other factor could be driven out of mind. He molded his thoughts around combat and nothing else.

"Like I'm going down without a fight!" Loren roared as that sensation blossomed in some dark corner of his mind. It was as if something had fit into place. As if something had clicked, and a ferocious smile spread across his lips.

As his roar echoed, he sliced through several trees, each as thick as an adult human neck. The bodies of the men chasing them turned to pulp and liquid in a scatter of splinters and fell to the ground.

With a bone-chilling grin carved on his face, Loren took off.

He shouldn't be that fast, Lapis thought. But now his physical might was enough to make even Lapis shudder.

If he were slicing with the sharp edge of his sword, it might have made sense. His weapon was sturdy, and it kept a good edge. His strength would still have been abnormal, but well within the parameters of what she was used to. However, Loren was smashing his way straight through the trees.

In this state, his weapon was practically irrelevant save for its weight, and the damage came from sheer brute force rather than any technique.

"This is..."

Lapis had seen Loren act this way several times before. He would go on a rampage, like a mad dog suddenly unchained, then drop unconscious when his body could no longer sustain the rage. The tremendous output put immense stress on his body, and he generally ended up in the hospital afterward.

For a moment, she doubted his choice.

No matter how powerful his attacks were, it was impossible to fight a prolonged battle like this. Wouldn't it all be for nothing if he collapsed now? Even as she thought that, a different possibility occurred to her, and she knew this was the best thing he could have done.

Their situation was only getting worse. The horsemen who entered the forest alongside them had been effectively wiped out, and Claes's party was rendered powerless. The missing villagers and soldiers were without sanity and gave chase like beasts in a state she did not even want to describe. Even if she could think up some plan, it was hard to imagine a clean outcome.

If Loren drops out now, we can use it as an excuse to get as far away as possible, thought Lapis. Of course, that meant that the problem would remain undealt with, but Loren would take care of their pursuers in his rampage. As long as Lapis didn't have to worry about men coming after her, she was confident she could do something about the peculiar space distortion Scena had mentioned.

If she let Loren do his thing, then she could shoulder his unconscious body and flee. The fact that he had purposefully called on his berserk state wasn't nearly as foolhardy as she'd assumed.

My only worry now, she thought, as she watched Loren smash through enemies and trees alike, *is if that he'll run out of strength before he can take all of them.* In that case, Lapis would have to take one for the team and start kicking.

If Loren were coherent enough to hear her apprehensions, he would have sighed and said, "They're not even your legs."

However, as far as Lapis was concerned, they were still connected to her, and they were the only legs she had available. She still needed ample time to psych herself up for it.

In the time it took Lapis to muster the necessary resolve, Loren converted man to meat again and again. He severed bodies and trunks with every swing of his sword, marching forth as though he had become a pure force of nature. As though he was the eye of a vicious storm.

Lapis watched everything around him fall to pieces in his wake until she noticed something peculiar. Loren's rampage wasn't supposed to last this long. The various energies within him—stamina, mana, and willpower—were usually drained by the force of it. A tremendous power came with a tremendous cost, yet the rampage he was on now seemed to thunder on and on.

"Does this mean..." Lapis immediately realized what was going on. It was Scena. Scena was using energy drain, the special ability of the undead to steal power from their surroundings and deliver that power to another, typically themselves.

Lapis had once taught Loren a self-strengthening method, but Loren possessed so little mana within him that he could hardly use it for long. Back then, Loren had compensated for this drawback through a continuous use of Scena's Energy Drain.

This had allowed Loren to continue expending mana to strengthen himself, but Lapis hadn't realized the very same method could keep him in his berserk state. With Scena feeding it, his rampage might not stop until his surroundings were completely devoid of life to leech off of. He wouldn't run out of strength, and he wouldn't falter.

Perhaps, if he was using more power than Scena could keep up with, he would eventually have to stop, but there was no telling just how long that might take.

"But that's bad in and of itself," muttered Lapis, panic lacing her voice.

Loren's rampages had a terrible kickback on his body. The only reason he was never hurt too badly was because he collapsed before barreling past the point of no return. However, Scena's Energy Drain sidestepped that safety valve entirely. Loren would continue to fight as long as there was a fight to be had.

If short bursts put him in the hospital, just how bad would it be this time? Lapis couldn't imagine it. All she could say for sure was that Loren was about to suffer more damage than ever before. Worst-case scenario, he might deal with the consequences for the rest of his life.

She needed to stop him—and this time it didn't take her long to steel herself.

"You can't, Mr. Loren! Stop fighting!"

Of course, it wouldn't have been a rampage if mere words could stop him. Lapis knew it was pointless, but she had to try. Loren didn't slow for even a second.

In that case, she would have to use force, but that was a problem in and of itself. If she fought with the intent to kill, Lapis was confident she would have the strength and skill to take him down, even as he was now. She had recovered her arms, which gave her access to much more of her natural strength and powerful magic.

No matter how skilled a mercenary Loren was, even if his armor was a gift from an Elder and his weapon from the forge of demons, Lapis knew she could overwhelm him from afar.

But she couldn't kill Loren. Her goal was to stop him from fighting before he incurred fatal recoil on his body, and it would be completely pointless to up and murder him instead. Unfortunately, it wouldn't be a walk in the park to subdue him without doing permanent damage. Loren was already accustomed to taking down foes stronger than himself, and that was before he went berserk.

If there was anything working in her favor, it was that Loren wasn't fighting with his head on straight. Even so, the battle experience drilled into his body might take her by surprise.

"Well. I'll just have to accept that we're both going to have a few bruises."

Knowing she couldn't subdue Loren without injuring him, Lapis resigned herself to a little pain. She circulated mana into her arms and began fortifying her body.

She considered taking up a weapon against Loren, whose sword was now little more than a corpse-making factory, but going in with some half-baked, improvised tree branch would only make things worse. She chose to face him with her bare hands.

Perhaps Loren's combat experience didn't encompass many unarmed opponents. His muscle memory wouldn't have much to say about fistfights, since he could pulp a fist fighter in one blow—at least, Lapis hoped this was the case, and she ran with that optimism.

When she wasn't holding back, Lapis could kill a human with her fists easily enough.

"That's enough, Mr. Loren! Please stop!"

The number of pursuers now was just about zero. Wood splinters and mounds of flesh littered the ground in their place, and Loren had created a decently sized clearing in the trees. Within that space, Lapis raced straight at him.

The poor footing wasn't enough to slow her charge. She raced over wood and flesh equally in her thunderous charge, but Loren was no slouch. Lapis spread out her arms, which had accumulated so much mana they shimmered like a mirage; obstacles parted from her in a wave as she dashed forward. Loren held up his sword as if he hadn't given the slightest thought to defense, and then he swung it at her.

It pained Lapis's heart that Loren attacked her. He never would have, had he been sane, but now that he was berserk, and Lapis had drawn his attention with her hostility, he saw her as nothing more than an enemy.

She promised herself that it was only until the battle was over as she crossed her arms above her head. Out of everything she could have done, she caught his blow with nothing but her limbs.

Sparks flew as the blade clashed with her defensive magic, and though Lapis barely managed to fend it off, she inhaled sharply at the sheer force. In her current state, she could catch the attack of a silver rank adventurer without flinching. Yet Loren's attack shaved through layer after layer of protection, and not only nullified her charging force, it sent her reeling back a handful of steps.

Even Lapis had to widen her eyes at that one. Her body was incomplete, and she was holding back so as not to kill him. But Lapis was a demon, and she hadn't thought there was a human alive who could put her on the defensive. She had furthermore instinctively realized she wouldn't be able to block him with one hand and had reflexively used two.

"You're outrageous, Mr. Loren."

Lapis was struck with wonder, but that didn't mean she was down for the count. No matter how powerful Loren's attack had been, Lapis had successfully blocked it. What came next would be a contest of pure strength, and if she could force him back, she knew it would be easy to incapacitate him.

Her two hands now clasped his sword; it was her victory to take. At least, it was until Loren began bearing down.

"You're telling me...I can't push him back?"

They must have made a strange scene, Lapis's arms locking with Loren's sword. She threw all her strength against him, trying to push the blade back, only to realize she was the one being crushed. Her braced legs were gradually being forced back, and Lapis looked up at the swordsman with renewed amazement.

She stared at the face beyond the blade—a face that couldn't recognize her anymore. If she let her guard down for even a moment, she would easily be sent flying back or forced to her knees by the pressure. Lapis stared into his eyes and muttered in awe, "Mr. Loren...you really are..."

6 From Restraint to Encounter

LAPIS KNEW that Loren's black blade boasted several enchantments. She didn't know all of them, but one of them would increase its abilities when pitted against magic. In short, Loren could block and counter spells with his sword, and Lapis had never thought she would see the day when she would regret that.

"This might be pretty dangerous."

His blade loomed right over her head. Although her mana-clad arms kept it from crashing down on her skull, the blade was slowly chipping away at her protective layers. Under its overwhelming might, it went without saying that Lapis couldn't move a muscle. She tried to push against it, but Loren's unleashed strength was greater than what she could muster while holding back. One wrong step and the sword would split her head open.

Lapis corrected her estimates of Loren's true strength. Naturally, she didn't intend to obediently wait for her head to be pulped; she poured even more mana into her arms until slowly the sword came to a stop, and then they were at a standstill. Eventually, she managed to push back by the tiniest degree.

There was no surprise on Loren's face as she resisted. He was thinking of nothing but battle and no longer had the capacity to feel surprised. Instead, he drew back his sword and readied another swing. He hammered down a blow with even more strength than the first one.

If Lapis took this one head-on, she couldn't be sure it wouldn't shatter her. She gave up on defending and used her mana-clad arm to parry. She felt immense pressure even in turning his blade aside, but she directed the sword's path as intended and used the opportunity to close in.

"This will hurt a bit, but please forgive me!"

There was a dull numbness in her right arm, the one she'd used to parry. Lapis gave up on using it properly and instead thrust it against his abdomen. In tandem with this, she took a strong step with her left leg, transmitting the resultant shock wave through her body and using her coiled muscles to amplify it. It passed through her shoulder, her arm, and finally into Loren.

A normal human would have suffered broken bones and incredible pain. Anyone else would have been left writhing on the ground. But Loren had taken the blow without defending. Surely it would have some effect.

"What the heck..."

Loren had definitely taken the full force of her attack, but regardless, he immediately jumped back to open distance between them and took a firm stance. She had channeled enough force to make any human faint, but it felt as if she had failed to hit her mark.

"That armor is from the highest order of vampires, so I expected it to have high defense. I didn't think it would be *that* tough."

Lapis's arm had hit Loren over his leather jacket, which had been a reward from an Elder vampire. It was made of layered pegasus leather with fine chainmail and shock-absorbing material sandwiched between each layer. Sure, Lapis had held back, but she had still mustered a good deal of force only for it to be completely nullified.

"How high-spec is that thing?!" she practically wailed in frustration.

Not that Loren paid her distress any regard. Having taken no damage, he went immediately on the counterattack. His blade sliced air, making the wind sing, and Lapis twisted to avoid it.

"I really hope we never have to fight for real, Mr. Loren."

After his slash, he immediately drew his blade back and safely regained his stance. In terms of both emotion and ability, Loren had become a man Lapis didn't want as an enemy. But that didn't mean the battle was over.

"What do we do about this, honestly? It's a real bother."

The head of a man went flying—a pursuer who had tried sneaking up on Lapis from behind. One of the survivors had gotten in a blind spot, but she easily took him out with one hand. By cladding her hands with mana, she imparted upon them endurance and lethality that could easily end a human life, yet none of this seemed to work on Loren.

When he had been an ally, an armor that could nullify her blows was more reliable than anything. Now that she needed to put a stop to him, she found herself wanting to cuss out the Elders, but Loren was the only one here. Lapis had nowhere to direct her irritation.

"Do I really need to get serious? One wrong step and I could kill you..." She wasn't too keen on that. But without putting her back into it, she was in danger herself. "You asked for it! Don't resent me if you die!"

Lapis imbued her arms with an amount of mana that dwarfed what she'd gathered before. On her first attempt, they had shimmered, but now they burst with blazing white light. Her ponytail and priest vestments fluttered, and the dirt and splinters under her feet exploded as she kicked off.

A purple light glowed in her eyes, which were theoretically prosthetics, and her usually serene face gained the sharpness of a blade. Loren readied himself to take her on, not faltering at the sight of her.

The slash that came next would probably be far more powerful than any before it. Lapis held her arms out to take it and destroy it head-on.

"I never thought you would be the first opponent I fought seriously, Mr. Loren!" *But that's not so bad,* she thought to herself and smiled.

Loren remained expressionless. Even the part of him used for talking was concentrated on the fight, and he didn't even let out a war cry to rally himself. As Lapis lifted her arms to take him, her vision was filled with a golden light so bright it was nearly white.

"What?"

Lapis stopped in her tracks, though Loren did not. Loren charged at her without even slowing down. Then he froze, sword hefted, and fell down on the spot.

She didn't think he'd run out of energy. Loren still looked like he had more fight in him, and she'd thought it would take a while longer. Sure, he would run out of strength quicker if Scena stopped supplying him with power from Energy Drain, but apparently, Scena rarely actually tried to see with his eyes. The only reason Scena had come out at all was because Lapis had smacked Loren and addressed her directly. Her voice didn't usually reach the Lifeless King.

All things aside, Lapis turned to the entity that had temporarily cut off her line of sight.

It, or rather she, had manifested perfectly between Lapis and Loren. Her pale blonde hair cascaded artlessly down her back, and her shapely chest was wrapped in a bright red strip of a top, with her stomach on full display. She wore the smallest of pants that nearly showed off the entirety of her thighs.

As a decently tall woman, her eye level was a bit above Lapis's, and upon seeing Lapis, she broke into a grin.

"Long time—well, short time, no see. Remember me?" The woman had a strange tone and a frank, open air. But what Lapis was most familiar with were the woman's purple eyes.

"You. You're..."

"Huh? Why, I reckon you're a bit different than the last time I saw you," said the woman. "So what, that's the real you, then? Tryin' to put on an act 'cuz you think it's all cool to be two-faced and the like?"

"I-it's nothing like that!" Lapis found herself protesting, her face bright red. She forced herself to return her tone to normal.

"Oh, back so soon? Then is *this* your real self? Guess it don't really matter." The woman smiled, or rather, she *smirked*.

Lapis spoke this woman's name, hesitantly and carefully. "Dark God of Gluttony, Gula Gluttonia..."

"You can just call me Gula."

"How could I act so friendly with you?" Lapis readied herself for battle.

Gula looked a bit morose. But she wasn't downtrodden at her core. She was just playing the part, and Lapis could tell that with only a glance. "Now that's sad. After I saved you and everything."

"You *saved* me?"

"Your boyfriend over there—Loren, was it? He was acting all strange, so I intervened."

Lapis was shocked. She was a demon, and it had taken most of her strength to face off against a rampaging Loren. Yet this "dark god" Gula had so gently and easily rendered him powerless.

"How did you do it...?"

"Well, that's a secret now, isn't it? I wouldn't mind telling you if you tried gettin' along with me... Umm, who were you again?"

"It's Lapis. I'm a priest."

"A priest?! You've gotta be kidding me! I see, you're an odd one, you are." Gula placed a hand to her forehead as if she was trying to remember something.

Though Lapis released her stance, she continued watching Gula's every move and asked the question on her mind. "What are you doing here?"

Gula looked like a normal woman, but her eye color was similar to that of a demon's. What's more, she was called a dark god and had been placed under a powerful seal. There was no way someone like her would show up if she wasn't looking for something.

After a moment of silence, Gula stared at Lapis and clapped her hands together. "You remember way back when? I said I wouldn't forget my debt to Loren over there. Well, I saw he was in a pickle and thought I'd help him out."

"That's the reason you're standing here right now. Not the reason you came in the first place."

One look at Loren would have told anyone he was in trouble, and Gula's reasoning was sound enough—whether Lapis believed her or not. However, that didn't explain why the dark god had come to this forest.

"Sharp girls like you are never popular."

"That kinda stings. Please don't go there."

The sight of Lapis's slumping shoulders must have been quite amusing, as Gula burst into hearty laughter. Once she was done, she wiped the tears from her eyes and said, "Well, to be real honest with you, I caught the scent of an old buddy around here. I thought I should go pick 'em up, so here I am."

"Oh, I see..."

"Not that I was expectin' much, but it looks like I hit the jackpot." Gula licked her lips as her eyes shifted away from Lapis.

Upon seeing this, Lapis braced herself. From the ring of trees outside the zone Loren had devastated, new figures began to emerge.

"These ones aren't quite to my tastes," Gula chuckled, hardly paying them any mind.

But Lapis, who had stooped down beside Loren's unconscious body, was less than pleased to see these newcomers.

Up until a moment ago, those that pursued them had acted strangely but still looked like your run-of-the-mill villagers and soldiers. These new enemies were clearly abnormal from the word go.

"Why are they buck naked?!" Lapis shrieked.

Every single one of them was a man rippling with muscle and, just as Lapis had decried, they hadn't a shred of cloth among them. Not only that, their eyes were bloodshot, and they breathed heavily as they looked at Gula and Lapis.

"I can't take it anymore... Mr. Loren, please do something about this..."

Lapis began slapping Loren in an effort to wake him, but he didn't react in the slightest.

"Hey, he's not getting up. Is he okay?" Lapis asked.

"Hmm? Yeah, about that." Gula seemed completely unperturbed as the maddened, naked men surrounded them. She spent a long moment lost in thought, as if all the goods on display didn't even phase her. But it seemed that thinking about it didn't lead her to an answer; she sauntered over to Loren and prodded at him with the tip of her foot.

"Hey!" Lapis protested.

"Yep, he's fine. Alive, at least."

Loren twitched ever so slightly. This meant he was alive, just as Gula had said, and Lapis clasped her chest in relief.

"Wait, this is no time to be thankful."

"Yeah, there's still all this hanging around."

"Don't say hanging!"

Lapis was trying her best to ignore it, but she couldn't help it when Gula put the shape into words. The men around them were certainly hanging.

Maybe I'll feel refreshed if I burn the entire forest down. Lapis indulged the dangerous thought, but before she could act on it, Gula began walking toward their foes, not wary in the slightest.

"Ms. Gula?"

"Take a little break, why don't you? I'll do something about all this..."

One of the men grabbed Gula by the shoulder before she had finished speaking. She could do nothing as the man forcefully shoved her to the ground. Gula's blonde hair billowed out, and Lapis was about to get up to help her, but Gula waved a dismissive hand.

"It's fine, all fine. I'm pretty strong," Gula said. However, the man holding her down by the shoulder had an unsightly sort of smile on his face as he straddled her.

"Have some class, would you?" Gula said, not even trying to stand. "You're killing my appetite here."

It didn't seem as though her words reached the man, but in the next instant, his upper half had completely disappeared.

"What just…?"

Even to Lapis, it looked as if half of a human simply vanished. His remaining lower body held its posture for a few seconds before spurting blood from its meaty cross-section. Once his legs fell to the ground, they vanished just as the rest of the body had.

"Filling, to say the least. But vile." Gula sat up off the ground. The naked men were still flocking to her, pouncing as if they hadn't just seen one of their members vanish without a trace. "Sure, I'll take you on."

Gula sluggishly stood without taking any defensive stance in particular. Just like that, several men lost their upper bodies, vanished as quickly as the first. It happened without warning, without reason. Their lower bodies followed soon after, and yet again, the other men didn't flinch.

"Now I ain't a picky eater, but I do like to savor a good meal."

A man who spread out his arms to grab Gula suddenly had nothing but meat and bones at both his shoulders. His balance crumbled with the loss of his arms, and as he fell forward, his head vanished. Then his torso, and finally his legs.

The ones around Lapis suffered similar fates. It was as if something was opening holes in them. Parts of their body would simply disappear until finally there was nothing left.

"What is...going on, pray tell?"

"Oh? Even you can't see them?"

Gula swung her right hand through empty space. Though Lapis strained her eyes to make out what was presumably there, all she could see was another muscular man blipping out of the world.

"The hell...is that...?"

"Mr. Loren?!"

The sudden voice at her side startled Lapis, and she grabbed his arm. He was prone on the ground, groaning as he struggled to pick his head up and watch with half-open eyes.

"Are you all right?! Can you move?!"

"I can't... What's going on...?"

After a struggle, Loren lifted his face, but without any strength in his arms, he couldn't go any further. Lapis flipped him over and sat him up.

"You suddenly collapsed. Do you know what happened?"

"I don't. It was like all the strength left my body... I was down in the dirt by the time I realized..."

"Yeah, sorry 'bout that. I had a bit of a nibble."

Gula's left hand was poised before her as if in solemn prayer, and she waved her right. This action proved sufficient to evaporate several torsos without a sound or any scrap of flesh remaining. Before what remained could even bleed, she waved her hand again and the leftovers were gone.

"Can you see anything, Mr. Loren?"

"It's...Scena's vision, I guess. I see...a whole bunch of giant mouths."

Propped up by Lapis, Loren could look around to see massive, transparent jaw-like things flying about. They would shoot out at Gula's orders and bite down on any of the men trying to attack her.

As for where their bodies disappeared to, he couldn't say. Since Gula was controlling them, they were most likely swallowed into some gullet of hers.

"Why can you see them, Loren?" Gula asked. "I guess that the one inside you must be lending you some eyes, huh? She must be quite somethin' if she can see my *Predators*."

Gula beckoned her many mouths to flock around her, and as they came to a stop, they each began to gnash their teeth.

"I savor tasty treats with this mouth up here, see." She pointed at her lips, running her tongue over them as her hollow eyes turned to the remaining men. "But it ain't too efficient when I just need to fill up."

Though her foes remained unmoved, Lapis saw that Gula's gaze was not what one would typically turn on other people. Gula was looking at the men like livestock, or a spread of tasty steaks already butchered and ripe for devouring.

"Anyways, when I don't want to use my own mouth, I use these *Predators*. Then I don't have to care too much about the taste, *and* it fills my stomach."

"Umm...going off of that, it sounds like those invisible mouths are connected to your digestive tract," Lapis hesitantly said.

Gula nodded like it was nothing. "Sounds about right."

"You...eat humans?"

Gula folded her arms and tilted her head. Around her, naked men were devoured one by one by mouths Lapis couldn't even see.

"Lapis, was it? You eat animals, don't you, Lapis?"

"For what it's worth..."

"Well, I don't really get it. Besides the taste, what's the difference between human meat and animal?" As she said this, Gula commanded a *Predator* to leave behind only the arm of its next victim, which she caught in the air. She held it up by the wrist and sunk her teeth in near its shoulder.

Her mouth was smeared with blood, and it took a few good chomps before she managed to tear away a good mouthful. She chewed a few times before spitting the blood and flesh onto the ground.

"It ain't tasty, but it at least takes the hunger away."

"The dark god of gluttony..." Lapis muttered, nervous.

Gula tossed the dead man's hand aside and wiped the blood from her mouth. "That's what they call me."

The slaughter went on without a scream. Gula's foes, defeated, devoured, and dead. It was one-sided annihilation, and though Gula would continue complaining about the taste, she seemed to be having the time of her life.

The mood changed soon after. Lapis held Loren up, only able to watch Gula's massacre from the sidelines. But the shift in the air caused her to tighten her grip.

"Are you trying to strangle me?"

"S-sorry. But this is..."

"Something's coming. That smell...it's getting stronger."

The smell Loren spoke of was the same sweet scent that had robbed him of his sanity and snatched away the minds of the soldiers and villagers who entered the forest.

That smell was suddenly growing stronger.

"You should put me out while you still can," Loren said. He could already feel his mind growing hazy.

With all his fatigue, he likely wouldn't be able to do much even if he did go into a frenzy. But he didn't want to do or say anything strange while in Lapis's arms, lest he die of shame.

However, Lapis responded to this proposal with a troubled look. After all, Loren was already in tatters. Gula had stopped his rampage, so he likely hadn't suffered any fatal damage, but the usual recoil had definitely wreaked havoc on his body.

"You're not going to die in one hit, are you, Mr. Loren?"

"Why are you assuming you're going to smack my lights out?"

If he just needed to fall unconscious, then a *Sleep* spell was enough. Even though Loren had a high resistance to magic, the magic would do its job as long as he didn't fight it.

"Sleep magic? Do you want me to?"

"Could you? I get the feeling it's gonna turn sour if you don't."

He wanted to be incapacitated before he did anything weird. But before he knew it, Gula was standing in front of him, reaching a hand to his forehead.

"What?"

"I'm returning what I nibbled on, with interest."

Gula grabbed Loren by the head. He could feel something

incomprehensible flowing in through her hand, and he tried to shake her off. But she wouldn't let go, and she held him with such force that he couldn't even turn his neck.

"What are you doing?!"

"There you go. Feel a bit better now?"

Loren knew he was no match for her, but once she let go of him and grinned, he thought he could at least get in a complaint. But he swallowed down whatever he was going to say; something was happening to his body.

The weariness he had felt from the moment Gula appeared was gone, and as for that haziness that had come whenever he took in that sweet scent, it was as though he couldn't perceive it anymore.

"I snacked on you a bit to calm you down," said Gula. "Now I've returned it and raised your resistance to this place, just a little bit."

Loren took care not to remove his eyes from Gula's smug face as he lifted himself out of Lapis's arms. He wasn't in pain, and his mind was clear. He was in nearly perfect condition.

"Are you all right, Mr. Loren?" Lapis asked, standing soon after him.

He nodded.

He didn't completely understand what Gula meant by a "snack," but she had likely eaten his stamina, or life force, or something of the sort to immobilize him. Still, she had clearly returned more than what she had taken, and she had indeed raised his resistance to the sweet smell on top of that. He couldn't see her motive.

"What are you thinking?" he asked.

"Well, that depends on what happens next. Worst case, I need you to have enough stamina to get away, or it'd leave a bad aftertaste in my mouth."

"Aftertaste?" Lapis repeated.

But Gula would explain no further. Instead, she took her eyes off of Loren and looked beyond the several naked men who still stood around them, staring. "If the smell's this strong, you've gotta be here. Right?"

"Gula, my dear... I am very sad."

Loren furrowed his brow at the sound of this sudden, booming voice. Lapis suddenly began to fidget and look around, as if she was fearful of what was to come.

"From the moment I opened my eyes, I simply wished to spread my love over these lands. Yet you devour my beloved prisoners of love. How very sad indeed."

Something's off, Loren thought as all the instincts he had fostered on the battlefield began to ring warning bells.

The words were spoken in the sort of tone he would expect from a brothel madame or old barkeep. At least, that was what his mind was telling him. However, a part of him refused to accept that. If he relied on his ears instead, it was the throaty, deep voice of a man.

"Hey, Lapis. Am I going crazy? I thought I just heard a man..."

"I think you're fine, Mr. Loren. After all, I hear a man too."

Gula's eyes were unmoving.

As something appeared beyond those naked men, Loren immediately found himself readying his blade, while Lapis fearfully held his arm.

"Love... It is beautiful yet unsightly, fleeting yet eternal, brittle, yet firm...and while it is unerring, it is also a mistake."

Though Loren found it quite unpleasant to look at the droves of naked men, he couldn't immediately say this was somewhere he'd rather be looking—for what arrived was like their essence. First off, he stood two heads taller than any of the other men, his black hair slicked back and lustrous. The face below that hair undoubtedly belonged to a man.

He boasted a mustache and cleft chin. Below that, his neck was as thick as a woman's waist, and this led into a sparkling, robust body of pure muscle. For some reason, he wore a shirt of black netting, which was practically bursting at the seams.

"Oh...wow..."

It hit the sheltered priestess Lapis so hard that she felt dizzy. Loren rubbed her back as he let his eyes go farther down.

The next thing he took in was a pair of low-rise pants, bulging to bursting from the muscles contained within. Every line of the man's leg muscles could clearly be made out from their constricting prison, and at the center of his hips was yet another bulge that left little to the imagination. At this point, Loren returned his eyes to the man's face.

"You've gotta be joking..."

"Oh, what heated eyes. Boy, are you interested in me?"

If this was a mental attack, it was incomparable to that sweet scent from before. Loren felt he might have lost his mind without the resistance Gula gave him.

"I don't blame you. I mean, just look at my body. A captivating little thing that anyone would pine for."

"Nah, I'd reckon he's takin' so much mental damage he can't move a muscle. Just look at that priest beside him; she's tryin' her best not to hurl."

"Ah, pardon me. No need to worry, my cute little priest. I do swing both ways."

Lapis quickly ducked behind Loren's back with a shriek, but even Loren wanted to get away as soon as he could. The only reason he didn't do exactly that was due to the pressure he felt—the same pressure as when he'd confronted dark gods like Gula.

He feared what one wrong move might do. Running wouldn't be that simple.

"Quit oglin' 'em," said Gula. "What are you even doing here?"

"Why, that's obvious. I'm building my love nest."

"To hell with that—you're indiscriminately calling people from all over. It's becoming a real problem."

"What does it matter? The more, the merrier. I am a philanthropist."

Loren contained himself and whispered to Gula, "H-hey. Who's he...?"

"Don't you have the least idea? I don't want to admit it, but *he's* one of *us*."

"Now that's just rude. What do you mean you don't want to admit it? Are you jealous of my looks? Wait, you weren't envy, were you?"

"Did you go senile while you slept? I'm gluttony. You're lust."

This ass of muscle was a dark god, and a god of lust at that. Both Loren and Lapis froze on the spot. Paying them no mind, Gula carried on with her explanation.

"Dark god of lust, Luxuria Luscharity. A lover unburdened by gender or age. From grannies and gaffers with a foot in the grave to...nothing worth talking about. Anyways, he's got a wide range of interests."

"There are no restrictions on love. It's a pleasure to meet both of you."

Hiding behind Loren's back, Lapis desperately held in a scream. Loren empathized to a painful degree. He couldn't move a muscle, stuck looking between grinning gluttony and winking lust.

7 Engage to Settle It

"WHAT EXACTLY are you here for? You didn't come here to tuck all my children into your bottomless stomach, did you?" Luxuria asked Gula.

Gula looked genuinely revolted as she replied, "Don't be daft. I wouldn't come all the way out here to look after your kids even if someone begged me to."

"Then what?"

Luxuria swayed his body upsettingly. Loren knew they had to do something, but he couldn't gather himself to speak. He instead resigned himself as Gula took point instead.

"Sit still, would you? You're scaring these two."

"Why are they so afraid? What did I ever do to them?"

"You don't have to do anything—just look at you."

My thoughts exactly, thought Loren. Of course, he couldn't bring himself to speak or nod, but he applauded Gula in his head.

"Now as for what I want, I want you to come with me," Gula said, cutting straight to business.

"I don't want to," Luxuria bluntly replied.

"Can I hear your reason?"

"I made such a lovely nest and gathered so many adorable children. Why must I throw it away to follow you?"

If he were able to speak, Loren would have suggested burning the forest down. If the influence of this god of lust remained in the villagers after they were released, they would make quite a mess of the world. He feared the future to come.

Luxuria turned away, pouting, while Gula let a dangerous smile spread across her face. "I could always use force."

"Just try it. I'll teach you just how powerless mere hunger is before love."

An unignorable level of tension stretched between the two dark gods. Something terrible was undoubtedly going to happen, and Loren slowly began to inch back while covering Lapis.

Gula locked her hands in front of her chest and snapped her fingers.

"What's a sex maniac got to teach me, eh?"

"You've got a nice body, if nothing else. I could hold you down and teach you the wonder of love directly."

"I'll tear you to bite-sized bits!"

The macho man with the cleft chin moved his fingers as if he was groping something—but Gula suddenly charged at him. There was quite a difference in physique, but Gula's arm shot out as if to say this was irrelevant. Her blow was caught in Luxuria's palm.

The impact created a thunderous boom, the sort that should never come from a collision of two living things, and it was

Luxuria who was pushed back by the clash. As Gula tried chasing him down, the naked men formed a wall before her.

It was a wall of sweat and glistening muscle, and Gula slammed her fist into it without the slightest concern. Though they were under the influence of the dark god's power, these men were not nearly as sturdy as their master. The one she struck burst to bits as though there had been an explosive inside of him, and Luxuria punched back through the blood splatter.

However, his fist never reached Gula. It was as if he had collided with something invisible, his knuckles locked in the air. Loren's eyes could perceive one of those transparent mouths quite literally sinking its teeth into his fist.

Though it held onto Luxuria's hand, the *Predator*'s fangs, which effortlessly tore through everyone else, couldn't even pierce through the dark god's skin. It stopped just barely pressed into the surface.

"Do you like the taste of my hand?"

"It's unpalatable, idiot!"

Gula manipulated her unseen mouths to attack. Luxuria used his free hand to tear away the mouth holding his fist, then began to fight off the assault of countless mouths with his bare hands.

A thunderous shock wave burst out each time mouth collided with fist, and waves of dust washed over the naked men, but while Luxuria had only two hands, Gula had more *Predators* than could be counted. Some dispersed when attacked, but it still seemed as though Gula had the advantage.

"You're cornered!"

"I don't think so. Try my *Lust Dance* on for size."

Loren presumed this would be something similar to Gula's *Predator*. However, the following scene was nothing of the sort. Luxuria took on a stance with his fists, and in the next instant, countless perfect copies of him branched off from his body and embraced the encroaching mouths in their hefty arms.

Just one Luxuria was enough, and Loren's soul cried out to see several. But he shielded Lapis and couldn't run. He had to endure this.

Each offshoot had an expression of rapture on their face as they disappeared, every one taking a mouth along with it.

Gula gritted her teeth. "You're using the same sickening skills as ever."

"They may have been mere copies, but your mouths went to heaven in my arms. Isn't 'sickening' a bit much?" Luxuria undulated his hips as he answered.

Again, Loren was filled with the urge to run. But he didn't want to draw the attention of either combatant. He was in Luxuria's realm, and he didn't even know if running would let them escape the reaches of that dark god.

We should have brought Claes, he thought, full of regret, though it was too late for that. Even if he was limited to women, Claes boasted a similar thought process to the dark god, and perhaps he would have been able to hold him at bay.

"This is getting nowhere," Gula begrudgingly conceded, seeing her *Predator* offset by *Lust Dance* once again. "We're evenly matched after all."

"You won't know until you try," Luxuria answered, though he didn't launch another attack. He too seemed resigned to their draw, or perhaps he hadn't been too motivated from the start. It seemed this was how a battle between dark gods typically ended.

However, Gula's next words took him by surprise.

"No way around it. I'll have that swordsman sub in for me."

"Hell no!"

"Gula, he may be cute, but when you can't do anything, I don't see how he could."

"You hold back, and I'll lend him a hand. Don't use your dark god authority. How does that sound? I lose if he gives up, and you lose if he hits you."

"So I'm supposed to concede if he lands a tingling blow? That's all? Fine, I'm good with that."

Don't drag me into this, Loren wanted to scream. However, the person dragging him in was also a dark god, and he didn't know which one would be more dangerous to offend. Rebelling was a matter of life and death.

"You're fine with those rules, then? If I win, you drop everything and follow me. If you win, you can make a love nest or pleasure garden or whatever." Gula's eyes turned sharp and she pointed straight at Luxuria. "Just don't leave this place until the world ends."

She made her way back to Loren. If he was her fighter, he'd at least earned a bit of complaining. "Don't get me involved with this," he mumbled, more timid than he would have liked.

"You want me to fight that guy forever? From here on out,

I'll have to stop worryin' about collateral damage. Are you fine with that?"

"Just for reference...if you two went at it seriously..."

"Well, the forest would be gone, for one, and the terrain would change entirely."

Loren shivered; it would be a battle on a level he had to prevent by any means necessary. But even knowing that, there was still something he had to say. "There's nothing in it for me."

Regardless of whether a village disappeared in a place that didn't concern him, or whether the landscape shifted, that didn't answer the question of why *he* had to fight some dark god of lust.

If there was no escaping it, he needed to draw out some benefit, or he might lose his life and get absolutely nothing in return.

"For you, eh...? Well, I guess it would be cruel to pit you against that guy without offering some compensation."

"In the first place, do I have any chance of winning?"

"Yeah, I get the feeling that one will work itself out... Wait, you keep talking about yourself. Don't tell me you're fighting him alone?"

"I can't have Lapis fight him, can I?" Loren pointed at the girl still clinging to his back and shaking.

Gula thought a bit, a conflicted look on her face, then patted him on the shoulder. "All right, I like you. It's pretty manly of you to keep the priest out of it. Fine, I'll make it worth your while."

"You'd better," Loren told her, dead serious.

In that regard, Gula seemed to brim with confidence. She struck a fist against her chest and declared, "Of course I will.

I may be a dark god, but I'm a woman of my word. Just leave it to me."

Gula never went into detail with regard to what she would give him. Loren tried drawing it out of her, but she simply assured him that it would be something nice and would say nothing more.

Loren wanted nothing more than to turn her down, but maybe that would just make her shrug and fight Luxuria instead. Dealing with the fallout of that would be a pain. For now, he decided to trust her when she said there was some merit in it for him.

As Loren readied his greatsword to face off against Luxuria, Luxuria locked on to him with a heated glance. Loren felt a chill in his stomach and spine and all others sorts of places as he glared back.

"Now that I've got a better look at you, you're not half bad."

From the bottom of his heart, Loren wanted to flee, but there was nowhere to run. He wondered just what he could have done to deserve this and received no response.

"First, let's see how far you can go in your base state," Gula chuckled.

Beside her, Lapis looked pale, anxious, and concerned, her hands clutched together at her chest as she watched Loren.

I guess I should be glad I didn't drag Lapis into it, he thought as he took his stance. "Let's go..."

"Come at me whenever and however you want." Luxuria beckoned him forth.

Loren kicked off and charged. Perhaps his desire to stay well away drove his tactics, as his first attack was a thrust using the full length of his blade. This meant the motion was small, and he could attack from as far away as his two arms and blade would allow.

However, he found himself gaping as his extended blade was simply smacked to the ground by Luxuria's palm.

His hands never left the hilt, but his posture crumbled as the force dragged him down. With his monstrous strength, Loren forcefully lifted the tip—which had stabbed into the ground—and tried slicing from below.

Once again, his trajectory was easily changed by a palm strike, and Loren allowed his blade to drag him to the side; Luxuria's fist appeared where his head had been a moment before.

As the parry sent Loren tumbling, Luxuria had stepped in and punched faster than he could perceive, yet Loren had somehow managed to dodge it. The dark god grinned—he followed Loren with his eyes without retracting his fist.

"Good reaction. I'm sure you make quite a lovely sound when struck."

Maybe this is what it feels like when prey is stared down by its predator, Loren thought as he prepared for his next move. If he was going to feel like that in any case, he would have preferred to fight Gula; in her case, his life would be in danger, but now, his spirit was in crisis.

Which one was better? He couldn't say, but he immediately went on the offensive. It was a horizontal slash, such that the blade would barely graze Luxuria. There was no need to properly slash him, as the agreement stated Loren simply had to land a blow.

He also remembered something about the strike having to tingle or whatnot, but whether it tingled was up to the man in question. In any case, the most important thing was to hit him. But this slash was deflected as Luxuria smacked the body of the blade.

This time, Loren had braced his feet, expecting to be swept away. Still, his attacks were deflected as easily as if he was swinging around a twig, and he cursed to himself.

After all, Loren's slashes were only possible with both the weight of his sword and the physical might to wield it. A shield would dent if it took that strike, and anyone who blocked with a sword would find themselves minus sword, hands, and arms. Yet Luxuria didn't break a sweat as he swatted the blade aside with his palms alone.

What am I supposed to do against someone so unconventional? Loren thought to himself as he unleashed his next attack. As was to be expected at this point, he was once again parried.

As he was running out of options, Gula called out, "Try strengthening yourself next!"

Loren recalled the sensation Lapis had taught him. He pictured the flow of something—presumably mana—in the deepest nooks and crannies of his body and brandished his blade. Now he could move with speed and power on a completely different level, but Luxuria didn't seem particularly surprised as he repelled the next swing of the blade.

Again, he didn't even scratch the skin of the god's palm, but something had changed. This time, Luxuria's hand reeled back after fending him off. Still, Luxuria's surprise lasted only a brief moment, and he quickly pulled his hand back to calmly deflect the second, then third slash.

"You've got the basics down, but you don't have enough *love*."

"Enough about love already. It's making me nauseous."

Loren gritted his teeth and hammered down a blow with all his might, only to be blocked by Luxuria's palm once more. He failed to even come close to landing a real hit. In the first place, Luxuria's hands were far faster than his sword. No matter how much power he put in, how fast he swung it, he would always be weaker than Luxuria, who wasn't weighed down by anything.

In that case, since his attacks couldn't damage Luxuria's palms, he would never be able to reach him.

"You wouldn't mind me counterattacking, would you? Don't worry, I'll nurse you back to health once you stop moving."

"Just leave me to die!" Loren practically shrieked as his swing was caught. Indeed, it was caught rather than parried, and as he was held in place, one of Luxuria's log-like legs hammered into his side.

Surprisingly, the impact was absorbed by Loren's jacket, and a good deal of the damage never reached him. But though he wasn't hurt, he was still thrown to the side and sent rolling across the ground.

"My, my, you're wearing some nice clothes. I was trying to finish up, you know?"

"You're a real monster..."

Luxuria's kick hadn't even been serious. He hadn't wound up or followed through, he'd simply given Loren a little love-tap. Loren was quite large and well-built, yet that kick had managed to send him, and his massive sword, ass over teakettle.

Luxuria was right—if Loren had taken that blow without the jacket, it would have been over.

"Next, I should aim for somewhere that jacket doesn't cover."

Loren could see the muscles shifting beneath Luxuria's pants as he pumped himself up for the next kick. Loren, of course, was not keen on falling unconscious under these circumstances and brandished the blade he never let go of even as he was thrown. Then suddenly, Gula was behind him, placing a hand on his shoulder.

"I'll help you a bit. Try strengthening yourself again."

Something flowed in through his shoulder—so much of that something that he worried if it would really be all right to accept. It was presumably Gula's supply of mana, and he immediately imagined it flowing through his body.

"You make it sound so easy."

Even with the mana of a dark god running through his veins, all Loren could do was slice and dice. And so he stepped forward to do just that, only to notice his body moving even faster than before.

He hesitated for a moment, but seeing as Luxuria was fast approaching, Loren couldn't stay flustered for long. He decided to shove off any doubts and swung his raised blade.

Luxuria was about to bat it away with his palm, as he had many times before. For some reason, for just a brief moment, the dark god's expression stiffened, and he dodged instead of parrying. Loren had little time to wonder why, shifting the trajectory of his blade, which had lost its mark and was on a collision course with the ground. He directed it into a diagonal upward slash, which was again evaded instead of defended against.

"Incredible. I didn't think you'd get that much better with just a little help from Gula over there. You're *wonderful*."

"Don't know what you're talking about!"

Loren took another step in and swung. Though he failed to connect, his blade sliced through the air, true to its course. Loren wouldn't give up; with another step, he drew a line from Luxuria's crotch to his head and backed off again as Luxuria dodged.

It seemed that Gula's strength meant his sword could no longer be repelled with a mere palm. He tried to give chase only to take a direct blow to the chest from an off-handed front kick, which carried enough force to send him flying back.

"You'll need to come up with something better if you want to hit me."

"Crazy bastard."

That counter kick had forced the air from Loren's lungs. He felt mildly nauseous, and had he taken it without the jacket, he suspected his ribs would have pierced his organs.

"Dammit! I don't feel any closer to him than before!"

"You can give up if you want to. You're welcome in my love nest anytime."

"I'd rather die!"

Loren sincerely thought he would. That was precisely why he raised his sword again when Lapis—who stood beside Gula—suddenly looked at Luxuria in horror.

"Then if Mr. Loren loses, he's going to get it on with...!"

"Why is *that* the thing you react to?!"

"I-I don't want that, Mr. Loren! Anything but that!"

"I don't want to either!" Loren replied as he decided to use the one thing he hadn't tried yet. He knew it was just about the last thing he could do. Although he didn't know if he would succeed, the situation would only grow worse if he didn't.

"Looks like you've decided to give me something. I'll take it with open arms."

Luxuria watched him, expression ecstatic, and Loren felt his resolve might crumble. He psyched himself up again and began to concentrate on the remaining mana Gula had supplied him.

He had completed this first step several times already, and he pulled it off rather smoothly; he used Gula's mana to perform self-reinforcement. Loren didn't know the specifics behind its inner workings, but he could pull it off through intuition and imagination. Perhaps Lapis was a good teacher, as he had never failed at this trick.

"That again? I expected a bit more from that fire in your eyes."

Perhaps sensing the mana permeating Loren's body, Luxuria went on the attack. Loren dodged the thrust of his fist and used the body of his sword to block his kick. He used the impact to put distance between them and silently reached out to Scena.

<I have a strange feeling about this, so I wouldn't recommend it, but...>

At present, Scena wasn't sharing his vision and didn't know what was going on outside. He usually felt sorry for her and tried to share his senses as often as he could, but this was one time he wanted to protect her innocent eyes.

Loren considered himself and Lapis too old to suffer lasting damage from these impactful scenes, but Scena—despite the nature of her existence—was quite a bit younger. Even while completely in the dark, Scena began providing him with mana.

What Gula supplied him had been powerful and vast, but he would run out if he wasn't careful. He asked Scena to use her energy drain to prolong the time he had left.

This would tremendously increase the length of time he could reinforce himself, as he had no way of knowing how long Gula's mana would last him.

"Are you aiming for a war of attrition?"

Scena targeted the trees around them, and since there weren't too many left standing, she also targeted the half-naked men littering the floor. Sucking energy from Lapis would have been akin to eating an ally, and as Scena was not a fully formed Lifeless King, there was no telling whether she could reap power from Gula or Luxuria.

Scena seemed to understand that Loren was trying to perform a powerful strengthening, so the effects of her drain were stronger than usual. The branches withered away right before his eyes, and the dead men shriveled.

With such a powerful supply, Loren thought of nothing more than the sword in his hands. He evaded punches and kicks, all of which would have been fatal, defending himself as he painted over his mind with nothing but thoughts of his foe and his blade.

Eventually, something clicked into place for Loren.

"You won't get far if you do nothing but defend… Wait."

Loren suddenly burst into a swing, and Luxuria leaped back with wide eyes. It was quite surreal to see his hulking build, which surpassed even Loren's, prancing about so nimbly, but Gula and Lapis's eyes were too fixed on Loren's attack to even pay it any mind.

It was so fast, it made it seem as if he had been holding back the entire time.

"What was that?" Gula asked.

"Yes, well…" said Lapis.

Loren roared. It was a great, earth-shaking sound, loud enough to shake the air itself, and Lapis found herself covering her ears and cowering. Gula stared with a stiff look on her face, and even Luxuria was frozen at Loren's sudden change.

With his sword held high, Loren charged. It was as though he wasn't aiming at all; no stroke followed a clean arc as his flurry of swings attempted to crush Luxuria with mass and momentum.

Luxuria managed to dodge the first few but quickly gave up on defending. Instead, he channeled mana into his hands to strengthen them and chose to match Loren blow for blow. His onslaught was simply too fierce to evade. Luxuria knew a strategy that relied on dodging wasn't going to cut it. Even with enhanced hands, it would be abnormal for Luxuria to be unable to fend this off with his fists, but Loren was even more abnormal than that.

"What's with this kid?! Isn't he a bit too fast?!"

In speed alone, Luxuria should have been faster. He didn't have to handle such an unwieldy weapon. And yet he quickly realized that the blade was being swung just as many times as, and just as fast as, his fists. Unable to bear it any longer, Luxuria began to generate blasts of magic from his knuckles to gain some distance, but even these waves of energy were sliced straight through.

"What's up with that?! If he could do that, he shoulda done it from the start! Hey, has he lost his mind or something?" Gula's voice was full of hope and expectations, seeing Loren push his foe back.

But Lapis simply stared as Loren fought with more force than she had ever seen before. Lapis had just seen his berserk state a moment ago, but when Loren confronted Luxuria, it was as though he had morphed into something else.

"Wait, is this..."

"What? Don't be a stranger, Lapis. If you knew he was hiding something like that, you could've told me." Gula patted her on the back.

In the next moment, Lapis reached out and grabbed her by the collar. Her eyes were wild as she said, "That's not it! This is completely different from what I knew about!"

"C-calm down a bit. They'll pop out if you squeeze too hard."

Lapis continued pulling up at the collar of her tube top, and Gula grabbed at her wrists, but her distress didn't seem to register to Lapis. Her head was filled with what Loren had just accomplished. "It's layering!"

"Layer...what's going on top of what?"

"He managed to put the rampage that earned him the name the Cleaving Gale on top of self-strengthening!"

Lapis had reached the crux of the matter. Thinking he had absolutely no chance if he fought normally, Loren had reached out for the berserk state that allowed him to surpass his own limits. Conveniently, he had recently learned to slip into it intentionally, and this time, he had gone berserk not in his normal state, but while in the strengthened mode Lapis had taught him to achieve.

He was already strong when he called on his rampage at his base level. And so, wouldn't he be considerably stronger if he powered himself up with an enhancement? The logic behind it was quite elegant.

"Ain't that a good thing? As a human, he's overwhelming a dark god, even if it's just in physical combat."

Luxuria could not effectively counter Loren's assault. If he lashed out with his arms and legs, countless blows would rain down upon him before he could bring them back. He could do nothing but defend.

Just from what Gula could see, Loren was pushing a one-sided attack, and Luxuria's defense was slowly falling behind. It was only a matter of time before Loren would get in a clean strike.

"This is terrible! His plain rampage mode has a kickback bad enough to knock him out! If he draws out even more strength, there's no telling how badly it will come back to bite him!"

Loren had to pay a price to build strength he didn't naturally possess. Now that he was even using the strength of a dark god's mana for his enhancement, that toll would be staggering.

"We need to stop him!"

"I *could* do that...but I think that would probably count as giving up."

"That's..."

If they put a stop to Loren now, then his odds of getting up after that would be despairingly low. If he could no longer fight, it would be the same as surrendering, and it would be Loren's loss.

Lapis wouldn't hesitate for a moment if there weren't anything on the line, but it was no exaggeration to say that a loss in this case would mean Loren's death.

"Worst-case, he could be beyond recovery... But if we stop him, his spirit will die..."

"You'd better decide quick... That idiot may be rotten, but he's one of us. It won't be easy to hit him... If we can provide an opportunity, then I think Loren could do it in his current state."

"An opportunity..." Lapis thought to herself.

She looked at Loren, who continued to swing, and Luxuria, who was barely managing to defend. She needed to do something that would take only Luxuria by surprise. She folded her arms in front of her chest and thought, then posed a question to Gula, who watched her with deep intrigue.

"Ms. Gula, Mr. Luxuria's sexual desire transcends all boundaries, correct?"

"I hate saying it aloud, but yes."

"Does he prefer men over women?"

"He doesn't. He's completely indiscriminate and loves everyone equally. Macho men and beansprouts, men and women, children and elders, they're all equal targets of lust to him."

"Hmm, that means..."

Lapis unfolded her arms and slipped them through her sleeves and under her robe. After fiddling a bit under her clothes, she wormed her hands through her collar, took a deep breath, and called out, "Mr. Luxuria!"

Lapis didn't wait for a reply. She only confirmed that Luxuria had glanced at her before tearing her collar open. The fasteners burst from side to side, revealing her upper half. What's more, as she rustled under her clothes, she had removed everything covering her chest and was left with nothing to conceal her bare skin.

Lapis's actions were so sudden, they took both Gula and Luxuria by surprise. Gula thought she was off her rocker, but Luxuria's eyes were taken in by the twin mounds of flesh and the colorful caps that she so boldly flaunted.

"My! What delicious-looking—"

Luxuria went for both men and women, and everyone was a target of lust. Even in the midst of battle, Lapis's body was more than beautiful enough to snatch his attention for a moment. But Loren was in a berserk state; even Lapis's nakedness didn't register to him.

As a result, the man who had nothing but battle on his mind now had an opportunity to strike.

The first blow caught Luxuria on the crown of his head. His magic defenses hadn't ceased, and his head wasn't split open, but as he staggered from the force, another strike was delivered to his nether regions from below. Luxuria screamed, but Loren's attacks didn't stop.

Perhaps Luxuria managed to maintain a minimum level of defense—the blade never bit into his flesh, but the air echoed with the sounds of steel rapidly hitting skin. Luxuria's throaty, shrill screams resounded as Lapis bashfully restored her clothing.

"That idiot. Even the way he loses is idiotic. I don't even know what to say..."

"He *must* be tingling after he's been beaten up that badly."

"Let's let Loren hit him a bit more before we stop him. Even so, you're pretty bold, Lapis. I don't know if you want to hear it from me, but you've got some nice tits."

"I-it's not like I'm losing anything by showing them off."

Just a glance at Lapis's face was enough to know she was putting on a strong front. Gula felt guilty teasing her any more than that; she made sure Luxuria was well beaten before nibbling on Loren's mana and stamina as she had done before, bringing him to a stop.

Epilogue
Reward to Recruitment

IS THERE ANY TIME happier than the time I spend asleep? Loren wondered.

There was no need to open his eyes. He could just spend his days resting in a warm bed. Of course, he knew he couldn't stay like that forever. He needed to wake up eventually, but at least he could enjoy the comforting warmth until someone came to rouse him.

When he tried to move, he noticed his sensations were dull. Perhaps he was in the hospital wrapped in bandages again—but something didn't feel quite right.

He was moving slowly, but he didn't feel anything restraining him. It was more as if he was enveloped in warm, viscous grease. Feeling somewhat irritated by it, Loren tried to wipe it away. He swung his hand, only to be met with something soft.

For some reason, he was distinctly aware that he had made contact with something. He suddenly felt a strangling sensation around his chest, and though he wanted to cling to sleep, he slowly opened his eyes.

The first thing he saw was a familiar ceiling. It was the same Kaffa hospital he had been brought to so many times—the sickroom, to be more precise. The memories from before he'd lost consciousness finally came back to him, and he sighed upon realizing he had troubled Lapis yet again.

He was, evidently, lying face-up on a bed. He tried sitting up, only to realize he couldn't. Loren immediately feared that the damage done to his body had finally paralyzed him, but then his gaze met a pair of purple eyes staring at him.

"Huh?"

Quite the farcical sound escaped his lips. The owner of those eyes had whitish-blonde hair, which spread out over his body as her face pressed into his chest.

What exactly is happening to me?

Loren belatedly realized that the warm, sluggish sensation came from the fact that he was being hugged—and that the one hugging him was naked, and he could feel her nakedness because he was also naked.

Had he been a woman, he would have screamed. He grabbed the head pressed into his chest and lifted it up, staring into those purple eyes again.

"What are you doing?"

He wasn't angry, as he knew he was dealing with someone far too scary to get angry at. When he calmly asked her what was going on, and Gula calmly replied, "I said I would make it worth your while."

"So this is the reward you were talking about?"

"Ain't it a sweet reward?"

Gula wrapped an arm around Loren's back, squashing the two voluminous bulges against him and letting them conform to his shape. Her chest was stuck against his, her legs firmly locked around one of his legs. It was as if she was using her entire body to ensure she was as close to him as possible.

"Now look here. I consider myself a normal man."

"You're a man all right. It was a bit stiff when you were asleep, but now it's standing tall and proud."

Loren awkwardly looked at the ceiling. Gula was grinning as though she could barely contain her laughter.

"You want me to eat you up or something?"

"Well, I couldn't call myself the god of gluttony if I let a human eat me."

Gula slowly raised her body over his, her purple eyes narrowing as a bewitching smile crossed her lips. Loren faintly feared for his life as she whispered in his ear, "So that's why...I'll be the one to eat you. And I'm gonna eat my fill."

That's not too bad, Loren thought. But in the next instant, there was a dull thud, and Gula's head shot sideways. He could guess what had happened as the dark god fainted onto his chest. As expected, he found Lapis peering into his face.

"Did I intrude on something?"

"You saved me. Maybe."

He would have been fine going with the flow. But he was at least aware that Lapis would have been in a bad mood if he told her that. Though it was a bit of a waste, he moved Gula's unconscious body aside and sat up. Lapis suddenly turned red and looked away.

"Put on some clothes."

"So you didn't just leave me here naked, then."

It was embarrassing to know Gula had stripped him, but he made sure not to show it. He glanced around for his clothes, found them by the foot of the bed, and grabbed them as Lapis looked the other way.

As he pulled his pants on, he asked Lapis, "So we made it out of there, right?"

"Yes, well. For what it's worth."

According to Lapis, she had somehow created an opportunity for Loren to strike the dark god of lust Luxuria while he was in his berserk state. It was quite terrifying how Loren had never managed to slice him despite all his unrestrained blows, but Luxuria had taken considerable damage. He had admitted his defeat and let himself be apprehended.

The villagers and soldiers under the dark god's influence had regained their sanity, and it had been quite a mess after that. As the man himself had declared, Luxuria's domain was lust, meaning everyone under his influence, man and woman, young and old, had indulged in acts that were not to be put into words, and they had suddenly regained their minds in the midst of it.

It would have been strange if there was no chaos at that point.

"That...sounds like hell."

"I don't even want to imagine it."

Naturally, Lapis had done nothing to bring the situation under control. She'd carried Loren—whom Gula had knocked unconscious—and left as fast as she could. Along the way, they'd recovered Claes and his party, and as they had passed through the village, they'd told Rose that the situation was tentatively resolved. She had then legged it all the way to Kaffa.

Additionally, the battle being fought near Rose's village had been resolved at around the same time.

The reason was unknown. However, according to Lapis's conjecture, quite a number of soldiers had been dragged away under Luxuria's influence; once they regained themselves, they realized what they had done and with who, and this ultimately created a situation where war was the least of anyone's worries.

It was an unfortunate incident, but there was little Loren could do once it was over. He simply prayed for the victims.

"What about the guy behind all of it?"

"I don't really know. Ms. Gula took him off somewhere."

They both looked down at Gula, whose eyes were still spinning from the blow to the head. They wanted a better grasp on the whereabouts of Luxuria, but Gula was a dark god as well, and not the sort of person they could draw information out of.

"I doubt she'll tell us."

"Yes, I doubt it."

Once that was decided, there was no further use thinking about it. They gave up on the matter. Perhaps they would meet the dark god of lust again, but not if Loren had any say in the matter.

"More importantly, Mr. Loren! You can't use what you used against Mr. Luxuria! Never again!" Lapis shoved her face close to his and glared at him until he nodded.

Knowing he would never normally get a hit on Luxuria, he had forcibly layered his rampage over his strengthening. It was a little late, but he was only now piecing together how terrible the recoil had been.

For one thing, his body ached all over. He didn't seem to have any broken bones, but he didn't know if that had been the case right after the battle.

"I treated you as much as I could, but some things simply can't be healed."

"Sorry. I'll be careful."

He knew he'd made her anxious, so he apologized sincerely. He would do it again if it was necessary, but he couldn't tell her that.

"So why's she here?" Loren pointed at Gula.

Lapis backed off a bit, cocked her head, and said, "I couldn't tell you why that thing is still around...for some reason, she just followed me."

"Aren't you being a bit cruel?" Gula suddenly jumped up, her uncovered bosom bouncing, and Lapis grabbed Loren by the ear as his eyes inadvertently darted southward.

"What am I supposed to do...? I'm a man."

"I understand that."

"So why are you here?" he asked Gula. "You didn't just come here to give me a reward, did you?"

"Well, there's that." She sat cross-legged and looked at him.

That's not a pose to do naked, Loren thought. As he was already clothed, he tossed his blanket over her.

"I'm interested in the two of you. I thought I'd hang around a bit."

Loren wanted to reply, *Sounds like trouble.* Then he considered the dangers of allowing a dark god to roam free. As far as he knew, gluttony, lust, and sloth had been unleashed unto the world. Yet he had had absolutely no idea where they were or what they were doing.

That wasn't a problem as long as they weren't making any trouble. However, if one of them was scheming something, then having another nearby would be the best way to get information and stay well away from any other incipient lust forests, or whatever.

Additionally, if they were going to keep one around, then Gula seemed like the easiest one to deal with thus far.

"Of course, when I'm hanging around, I'll help out with this and that. I'll be good. All I need is food and lodging."

"In your case, won't your food costs be extraordinary?"

"But I think I can earn you quite a bit too. How about it?"

Loren looked at Lapis, troubled, but she silently closed her eyes. It seemed she was leaving the decision to him.

He thought a bit more, then answered, "Don't cause any trouble."

"I'm looking forward to the food," Gula said with a slovenly smile.

In contrast, Lapis held a hand to her forehead and reported, "Mr. Loren, these past few days, Ms. Gula has already emptied ten dining halls. Please keep that in mind. I already paid the bill."

Suddenly, he felt like driving her away. "Add it to my debt," he managed.

"No, I'll split the cost with you."

"Ah ha ha. Well, I seriously will earn money for you. Let's all get along, eh."

Gula laughed, so carefree, her head bobbing and her breasts swaying. Lapis looked at Loren sullenly as his eyes were sucked in and pinched at his cheeks. He didn't know whether this had been the right decision or not, but it *was* decided. He shrugged.

Bonus Story: From the Notes of a Certain Priest

HELLO, LAPIS AGAIN. For some reason, I get the feeling that I grow less normal every time I proclaim myself a normal priest of the god of knowledge. I thought repetition would enhance the word, but strangely, that does not seem to be the case.

Putting that aside.

This time, it all started with a rather strange rumor. Several villages all vanished at once; it would have been even stranger if that hadn't become an issue. I would really like a heartfelt apology from those Elders.

Yes, I know it will never happen.

That wasn't all, though. As it turned out, the country in which we set up our base of operations had gone to war with its neighbors. Knowing there was a war nearby, I was a little worried about Mr. Loren.

He was once a skilled mercenary, so it wouldn't be strange if he gave up adventuring and returned to his former occupation. But worrying rarely accomplishes anything. He said he wasn't interested when I asked him directly—a real relief, if you ask me.

Not that it really matters. If he said he wanted to return, I'd just have to march with the army as an ordinary everyday priest. But it would have been rather inconvenient to give up on adventuring after we've already established ourselves, so perhaps the fact that Mr. Loren is staying away from wars is indeed quite a blessing for me.

However, even if he wasn't interested, nearly every job on the guild board had to do with the war. I can understand that war is no time to kick back and gather herbs or hunt monsters, but I had to wonder if it was really all right to do away with everything else.

In any case, Mr. Loren's empty wallet meant he had to work to live. I didn't want much to do with the war, so I needed to carefully select the jobs I would recommend to him.

Long story short, there were no good offers. Perhaps it was understandable, with the war and all, but it was quite a bother. They were all either too dangerous or paid too little.

That was when Mr. Claes entered the fray. It seemed it was about a woman again, and he was no doubt up to no good. I was convinced of it, but it wasn't like we had anything better to do. If Mr. Claes could solve our money troubles, I felt it would be a little easier than taking on any of those other jobs.

But is it just me, or is Mr. Loren a bit too soft on Mr. Claes? I'm not suspicious about their relationship or anything, but perhaps mercenaries are the sorts who put in way too much effort to make comrades of any colleagues that aren't complete villains.

For a moment, I regretted treating Mr. Claes too harshly. Then the story came out, and it was indeed about women again. Mr. Claes had been seduced by a widowed village chief and took on a job he would lose money on. And because he wasn't sure he could do it with his party alone, he had turned to Mr. Loren.

This amazed me on two fronts. The first, which went without saying, was Mr. Claes's relations with women. The other was the village chief, who audaciously submitted a job to the guild that she knew would never turn a profit for anyone involved.

I was concerned about the future of a village led by someone who couldn't perform basic math, but it had nothing to do with me. Perhaps she was counting on there being several Mr. Claeses among the adventurers.

In the case of the latter, that would make her quite the schemer. However, the job was far less dangerous than scouting for the war, and so we took up the task after making some unreasonable demands from Mr. Claes.

Apparently, Mr. Loren planned on taking it for twice the pay Mr. Claes was offering, but that wasn't the right way to go about it. I presented three times the cost, knowing it was far too much, and Mr. Loren managed to settle the matter by haggling it down ever so slightly. I even felt a sense of gratitude from Mr. Claes, and thus everyone was happy.

Starting out with unreasonable terms is the basics of skillful negotiation.

Incidentally, our necessary expenses came out as a separate fee. Mr. Claes was footing the bill, so I considered using the opportunity to nab the expensive sleeping bag and pillow I'd been eyeing, but Mr. Loren stopped me. He said bad deeds would come back around, so I had to be a bit restrained.

It is in a demon's nature to be thorough whenever you have the advantage, but I gave in for Mr. Loren's sake. Being stubborn would only lower his opinion of me, and I am aware that it's sometimes important to know when to give up.

Now about that quest. The job involved delivering supplies to a village. All the villagers involved with the transport were women. No wonder Mr. Claes was hooked.

If I'm recalling correctly, Mr. Claes managed to get his comrades on board by vaguely telling them it was a job to save a village in need, but they exploded at him once they learned the truth. I knew it would be pointless no matter how many times they kicked him—the problem will never resolve itself until they cut ties with him...or cut him physically.

Even there, Mr. Loren had Mr. Claes's back. There should be a limit to being a good person. Did he have an air about him that made it impossible for Mr. Loren to leave him be? Or did Mr. Loren sympathize with him a bit more, being a man? In any case, I think Mr. Claes should take a page out of Mr. Loren's book, and meanwhile even if it is just ten percent of what Mr. Claes has, Mr. Loren should develop a little more interest in women.

After this and that, we set off. Our client was Ms. Rose, the lady chief of the village, and she was absolutely no good. In short, she was well aware of her appearance and its effects on men, and she had already used it to lure in adventurers like Mr. Claes and put them to work on the cheap several times before. She was a repeat offender.

I wondered whether the fact that her convoy was all women was part of her ploy. What irked me most was how she tried to sink her claws into Mr. Loren as well—though she was quickly turned down.

You cannot underestimate Mr. Loren's self-restraint. He has me right beside him and never does anything to me. There's no way someone on Ms. Rose's level would ever be able to sway him.

No, a part of me feels it's less his self-restraint and more that he's just a blockhead, but...getting back on track, there was a bit of an incident with bandits, but the supplies reached the village without an issue.

Mr. Claes and his knight friend, Ms. Leila, were able to resolve the incident alone, and both proved to be quite adept. Incidentally, I received confirmation that Mr. Claes's backer is Waargenberg, the nation that encompasses Kaffa. He's surprisingly careless and loose-lipped.

Anyways, once we reached our target, it was clear something was strange. Apparently, men and women of all ages were disappearing for reasons unknown. Contact had also dried up with the neighboring village or something.

The transport convoy wasn't all women due to the village chief's scheming, but because apparently, all the men had disappeared before the women did.

Of course, this was irrelevant to us, and there would have been no problem with ignoring it, but Mr. Claes could not turn down a request from a woman, and Ms. Leila could not abandon the weak. Just like Ms. Leila, Mr. Claes's priest comrade, Ms. Laure, said she could not abandon those in need.

As a fellow priest I was unable to say, "Just abandon them," and had no choice but to hop aboard. Mr. Loren toughed it out, insisting he wouldn't do it for free, and Ms. Leila proposed a monetary reward from all those who had already accepted; this meant that not only did I take on the job for free, I even had to pay Mr. Loren to do it.

Did I do something bad? Is this my punishment? I don't remember ever offending the gods enough for this.

Perhaps those thoughts showed on my face, as Mr. Loren came around later and said he would return the money I gave him. I had to turn him down, but I made him promise to treat me instead. That cleared my head a bit. Afterward, Mr. Loren threatened Ms. Rose a little, as she had not even tried to support our expedition, which was again quite refreshing.

We headed to the neighboring village to find it just as abandoned as expected. From food to valuables, everything had been left as-is, and it was all free pickings, but I had to restrain myself with Mr. Loren watching. He is quite an honorable person.

After spending a night in the abandoned village, we had a run-in with Waargenberg's soldiers. They informed us of a good number of deserters from the army and asked us to accompany them. It didn't take long before something strange happened.

Of all things, Mr. Loren, Ms. Ange, and everyone else seemed to come under the effect of some strange phenomenon that turned their heads into a field of flowers. Perhaps that may sound misleading, but to be clear: it put them in a state where they could barely hold back their carnal urges.

Luckily, Mr. Claes was all right, but Mr. Loren was down so bad, he had to smack himself to keep it together. I considered knocking him out, but then it would have been quite troublesome to move him around, so I had him temporarily switch out with Ms. Scena instead. It was quite upsetting when she called me, "ma'am," with Loren's face.

Mr. Claes's party had to drop out there. Although Mr. Claes, who had the makings of a hero, was not affected, his comrades were, and on top of that, I went a bit too far and rendered them immobile. With little choice in the matter, I operated alongside Ms. Scena in Mr. Loren's body, and for some reason, the people attacking us were all naked from the waist down.

I had no choice but to run. I mean, I am a maiden, after all. I dashed through the trees with Ms. Scena, but along the way, Mr. Loren took over and went on a rampage. He regained control and annihilated our pursuers, but he could no longer distinguish friend from foe. I was forced to engage with him.

Amazingly, with his sword and his protective gear from the Elders, Mr. Loren proved to be a threat even to me. I nearly fought him a bit seriously, only for the dark god of gluttony, Ms. Gula, to suddenly appear and interrupt us.

I was thankful that she knocked Mr. Loren out for me, but that left a few questions, and I had no time to seek their answers. After all, the next batch of pursuers was *completely* naked. Such indecency right before an innocent lass... Even I had to cry out at that point. It was difficult even for a demon's spirit.

I mean, I haven't seen one since I saw Dad's as a little girl... In any case, the important part is, I am a prim and proper maiden who refuses to trace her memory to remember what her father's looked like.

With a backward glance at me, Ms. Gula began using her authority of gluttony, which took the form of *Predators* that devoured her foes until nothing remained. Gluttony apparently recognizes humans as food.

It turns out I did learn something.

Putting that aside, Ms. Gula splendidly massacred our assailants, but that was not to be the end of it. The culprit who had driven Mr. Loren and everyone else out of their minds was approaching.

I considered knocking Mr. Loren out again, but Ms. Gula did something that eliminated the need. I prepared myself for whatever was coming, and what appeared was...to be blunt, extraordinary.

Umm, honestly, I was feeling a little sick at the time and took so much mental damage that Mr. Loren had to intervene, so I'm not confident I can properly put it into words.

For what it's worth, he looked humanoid. But he was covered in bursting muscles all over and wore a transparent black net shirt. His low-rise leather pants, which hung as low as possible, and his general fashion sense made me question if something was wrong with his head.

His appearance already made me dizzy, but his statements didn't make it any better. Rather than struggling to understand, it was more that I *refused* to understand. When it all came together, it was incomparable to the loss of sanity he had cast on Mr. Loren and the others.

Perhaps a human city would have fallen to his simple existence. Maybe even a demon country... No, I shall retract that statement.

A completely normal demon like me may have taken damage from his presence, but the not-so-normal would most likely have laughed it off. My mother, for one, would have just ignored him. I am lacking in experience.

Back then, I hoped it was a joke, but that being turned out to be a dark god just like Ms. Gula: the dark god of lust, Mr. Luxuria. When it comes to lust, wouldn't you usually imagine a sexy, voluptuous, older woman? Who benefits from having a greasy muscle man in charge of that?

If this was the work of a god, then that god was certainly crazy. At the very least, it had nothing to do with the god of knowledge that I serve. If my god played even a small part in it, I would never excuse them. Rather, please save me. If you can, please erase these memories from my head.

When I write these things, it's usually several days later, and just what I can remember, but I see it in my dreams. I've dreamed of it several times after that incident. I wake up screaming in the night—a demon having nightmares.

The fear comes back to me when I look up at the window—just how deep of a mark did it leave? Is this one of those curses?

The sort that plague one's head until the moment of their death? Will I be released if I die? Is that what it will take? Tell me.

Am I already beyond salvation? If not, then what can I do to escape it?

Yes, let's take a deep breath. It's pointless to write anymore.

I don't want to falsify my own records, so I'll leave what I've put down so far, but I've illustrated something quite unsightly. Those memories nearly came back and made me end myself.

It's all right now. Yes. I am normal.

I am fine. I am fine. I am fine. I am fine. I am fine. I am fine.

I am still immature.

When I think of it like that, the swordplay and combat abilities with which Mr. Loren defeated the dark god of lust were incredible, but his mental fortitude—that allowed him to keep his eyes locked on that dark god the whole time—is truly greater than mine.

I felt a chill when he entered his berserk state from his self-enhancing mode. It was certainly effective, but I knew the burden it placed on his body would be enough to put his life at risk.

But even if I told him that, I know Mr. Loren will use it anyways, if he has to.

Mr. Loren managed to defeat Mr. Luxuria with his hard work, and that led us to finding the missing villagers and soldiers. They had all been dragged back to Mr. Luxuria's love nest. A sickening end to a bizarre tale.

Incidentally, I helped out a bit by, ah, taking a load off my chest, let's say, but I don't want to talk about it. It was necessary. I was less impacted by the shame than by the fact that Mr. Loren didn't even look my way. No, I wasn't trying to show him anything, but for him to have absolutely no reaction is...

I made an opening for him to attack Mr. Luxuria, so it wouldn't even have worked if he had stopped to look. How should I put this? It's just a little frustrating.

As per usual, it was a mess after that. First, there was chaos as Mr. Luxuria's influence wore off. I somehow managed to slip away, carrying Mr. Loren's unconscious body, to meet up with Mr. Claes and leave the forest. Upon returning to Kaffa, I left it to Mr. Claes to report the results and immediately filled out the paperwork to get Mr. Loren into the hospital.

As I breathed a sigh of relief, I found out that Ms. Gula was going around town, visiting dining halls, and putting it on our tab. I hurriedly tracked her down and caught her, but I had to pay the bills anyway.

Though I could have left her be, it would be incredibly dangerous to leave a dark god to her own devices...and Mr. Loren and I were the only ones she claims any relation to.

Then I visited Mr. Loren in the hospital, wondering why it had to come to this, only to see Ms. Gula's naked body overlapping his. Before I knew it, I had smacked her without holding back whatsoever, but as expected of a dark god, she was quickly back up on her feet without major injury.

According to her, she is interested in us and wants to work together.

I fully intended to turn her down, but I couldn't, considering the danger of unleashing her as a free agent. She would be quite reliable as an ally, in any case, so we took Ms. Gula as a new party member.

Even so.

From a third-party perspective, with one man and two women, our party is beginning to look like Mr. Claes's—though one woman is a demon, and another is a dark god. I know I'm a part of it, but I feel a bit ashamed. As I set down my pen, I pray Mr. Loren doesn't think about it too hard.